LEGACY OF THE LAKE

JUDITH HARTSOCK

Rising Tide Press
PO BOX 30457
Tucson, AZ 85751
520-888-1140

Copyright 2001 Judith Hartsock

Without limiting the rights under copyright reserved above, no part of this publication may be reproduced or transmitted in any form or by any means without prior written permission of the publisher.

Printed in the United States on acid-free paper.

Publisher's note:
All characters, places, and situations in this book are fictitious, or used fictitiously, and any resemblance to persons (living or dead) is purely coincidental.

Cover art by Jude Ockenfels

First Printing: May 2001

    Hartsock, Judith
    Legacy of the Lake/Judith Hartsock

ISBN 1-883061-47-4

Library of Congress Control Number: 2001 132069

Dedication:
 To Celyn who forgave me, to Noreen who encouraged me, and to Monita who always, always loved me.

Judith Hartsock

LEGACY OF THE LAKE

JUDITH HARTSOCK

Chapter One

Clary was snatched from sleep by a sound on the roof, a tree branch falling, or perhaps one of the feral cats who roamed the woods. Instinctively, she reached across the bed for reassurance from Barbara, and then, remembering, pulled her hand away and pushed the bedclothes off.

Lucy, her old retriever, lifted her head and lumbered across the room, her claws clicking on the hardwood floor.

"Time to get up?" Clary asked.

Lucy yawned.

Clary pushed herself upright, scooted to reach the floor with her left foot, and dragged the right in its cast across the mattress. It settled like a stone on the floor. She struggled into a robe and reached for the crutches she'd been lugging around for the past two weeks.

She'd broken the foot jogging to lose weight. In her zeal, she'd overextended herself and stepped in a pothole, collapsing on the road in excruciating pain. Luckily, Norma Latham, one of her neighbors, had come by to ferry her to the emergency room in Metcalf, some twenty miles away. The doctor had predicted six to eight weeks for the foot to heal. She wondered how she'd stand it.

Swinging into the crutches, Clary caught sight of a photograph on the wall across the room, a photograph of herself and Barbara taken on a vacation in the Napa Valley. They'd posed outside a winery, giving their camera to a passerby. Grape leaves snaked up the brick wall behind them and curlicued over the tops of the stacked wine kegs. Even then, Clary had carried a few pounds more than ideal for her five foot five inches. Her round cheeks were exaggerated by a carefree smile, her dark complexion pink-tinged from the sun. She'd worn her hair longer then, broom straw straight and black as any Iroquois ancestor. Green eyes hinted at the Irish portion of her lineage.

Barbara stood behind her, a good head taller, one arm draping Clary's shoulder. At forty-seven, she'd earned the spritz of gray hair that threaded the blonde. A wayward strand clung to one cheek, held fast by the wind. She'd worn sunglasses that day, and Clary had wished a hundred times that she could reach into the picture and take them off. She had loved Barbara's beautiful sapphire eyes.

The photograph had been taken four years ago on what had turned out to be their last vacation together. A year later, Barbara was diagnosed with pancreatic cancer, and six months ago she had died. Clary still ached every day, missing Barbara, missing her main reason for waking up each morning.

At eight o'clock, the thermometer in the kitchen already read seventy-five degrees. And this was only June. They'd have triple digit temperatures by July. Clary dreaded the coming heat. It was hard to imagine what it would be like to swelter in the house with a ton of plaster on her leg.

She plunked down a bowl of food for Lucy and made a pot of coffee. Her doctor had advised her to drink decaf, cautioning that at forty-two she needed to take better care of herself. Decaf had been well and good before the accident, an easy sacrifice to make with her bones intact and life running smoothly. Now, she felt entitled to every indulgence.

She filled her cup and stumped out onto the veranda. The sky was clear, the air sweet with the scent of pine and wildflowers. In a couple of hours, the lake would be filled with swimmers and boaters, the shoreline speckled with picnickers. From the steps, she had a clear view of the boat house, the two rental cabins, and the swimming pool, all surrounded by pines and oaks. The only thing disturbing the peace and quiet was the sound of bulldozers on the opposite shore. She tried to blot the construction project out of her mind as she looked out over her inheritance, her legacy from Barbara.

* * * *

They had met in San Francisco, where Barbara was teaching at the university and writing novels in her spare time. Clary was working as a receptionist at a law firm. The job was unrewarding and paid poorly. Even with Bill's child support payments, she barely had enough money to sustain herself and her two children.

Living in these dire circumstances, Clary wished every day that she could go back and change the past. If only she had recognized her sexual orientation earlier in her life. If only she hadn't married Bill Ingersoll when she was just eighteen. If only she hadn't started a family. If only, if only, if only.

But, of course, there were reasons for everything that had happened in her life, some of them good, some of them bad. Marrying Bill had definitely been a bad idea. It had blossomed from her desire to create the kind of home she had never known as a child, having been given up by her mother to live in a series of foster homes. She should have known that marrying a man she'd known less than a year and moving into his apartment, and his bed, could not make up for what she'd missed.

Having two children, one practically right after the

other, had also been a bad idea. There was no question that she loved Richard and Karen, but, as she quickly realized after her divorce, she was ill-equipped to care for them.

As to her sexual orientation, well, that was something over which she had no control, either in its existence or in her recognition of it. She'd had hints over the years, but the realization hadn't begun to take shape until one day when she and Bill took the children to the park.

They'd spread a blanket on the grass to loll in the sun, while Karen and Richard, ages three and five, romped on the playground equipment. Bill had taken his shirt off and sat cross-legged, reading an auto parts catalog, leaving Clary to keep her eye on the kids. She hadn't realized that Bill had taken his eyes off the catalog and was watching her until he said, "What's so interesting about that woman?"

Clary quickly turned her attention to her husband. "What are you talking about? What woman?"

"That jogger warming up over by the swing set. You've been staring at her for the last fifteen minutes."

"Have I?" Feeling inexplicably guilty, she'd pulled her gaze away from the woman and looked at her husband. "I didn't realize I was staring."

"Well, you were. Better keep focused on the kids. It wouldn't take any time at all for them to break their necks on the jungle gym."

After Bill returned to his reading, she glanced in the direction of the jogger again. What was so interesting about her? What *wasn't* interesting?

For the next several weeks, Clary was visited by a string of memories, exciting and disturbing at the same time: the crush she'd had on her tenth grade math teacher; the female movie stars she admired and her failure to understand why her friends went gaga over the male stars; the time she tried to fondle her best friend's breasts at a sleeping party when she was twelve.

As she slowly processed all these bits and pieces from her past, Clary could only come to one conclusion. She was a lesbian. She shared the information with Bill one night after she'd refused to have sex with him for the third time that week. They'd started divorce proceedings the next day. A week after that, she moved out with the children and found an apartment.

Bill made his child support payments religiously and took the children home with him every other weekend. The payments continued, but, as time went on, the time he spent with Richard and Karen became less frequent. Inside of three years, he stopped coming for them altogether. Shortly after that, he moved to New York and married his childhood sweetheart. Except for the checks he sent, neither Clary nor the children heard from him again.

Clary's computer skills were decent, and she had a pleasant personality, so it didn't take her long to land a job. But she soon realized that she'd need a college degree to move on to something better. She'd enrolled in night courses at the college, and Barbara was one of her instructors. Their attraction had been instantaneous and strong, and they had moved in together almost immediately.

The following year, Barbara's parents were killed in an automobile accident, and Barbara had inherited their home in Metcalf and the lake property, which Barbara's father had purchased with retirement in mind. With two novels already published and a third near completion, Barbara had cut her teaching hours and moved Clary and the children with her to the lake.

The locals remembered Barbara as an attractive, slightly tomboyish teenager who often visited Lake Lassiter with friends in the summer. They seemed delighted when she returned as an adult to take up residence. Dan and Marge's girl, a real live novelist, right here in Lake Lassiter. Their attitude changed when they realized that Barbara had brought a woman to live with her. Barbara and Clary made no effort to hide the nature of their relationship, and out of respect for the Hadleys, most people had been civil. Unfortunately, their nearest neighbor, John Munger, had proved to be truly Odd homophobic, as had Ellen Graham, the owner of the local inn. Regardless, the thirteen years that Barbara and Clary had lived at the lake had been the happiest years of Clary's life.

* * * *

Looking out from the veranda now, Clary wondered what
condition the cabins were in. Since the broken foot, she'd said goodbye to two sets of vacationers and had made no effort to clean up after them. She called Lucy and trudged down the path to assess the situation.

The retriever loped ahead, seeming to know their destination. Clary followed on her crutches, noting the kneehigh scrub along the way. It called out to be leveled before the summer heat baked out all the moisture. In these mountains fire threatened constantly, even into fall. The swimming pool needed attention too. Before the accident, she'd cleaned it religiously and tested the water every day. Now it was murky and mottled with algae. She hated to spend the money, but it looked as though she'd have to hire help.

She entered Tahoe first, remembering how Barbara had insisted on names for the cabins, Tahoe and Telluride. She'd even made wooden signs to go above each door. Clary smiled at the picture she still had of Barbara's lanky body hunched in concentration as she carved them in front of the fireplace one night. Like everything she attempted, the results were wonderful.

The mess inside Tahoe included clots of mud in the bathtub and sticky spills across the vanity. The bedclothes lay in a tangled heap on the floor, and trash and empty bottles littered the place. Telluride was in the same condition, causing Clary to wonder what gave people the idea they could
behave like pigs in rented rooms. Overwhelmed with the enormity of cleaning up, she called Lucy and began her slow climb to the house.

On her way, she made a detour to her mailbox up on the road. She hadn't checked it in days, and the accumulation spilled out the front. Propping her crutch against the box, she balanced on one foot to remove the contents. Along with the inevitable junk mail, she counted four bills, including one from her insurance company. Her spirits plummeted when she opened it and saw what she owed.

Before breaking her foot, Clary had worked at the hardware store in Metcalf. The pay wasn't great, but it supplemented what Barbara earned in royalties and the rent from the cabins. With two cabins vacant and her checking account almost depleted, she had no idea how she would manage this month.

Feeling as if the weight of the world rested on her shoulders, Clary continued her slow ascent to the house. As she mounted the steps, the phone began to ring, and she realized
she'd forgotten to activate her answering machine. She snatched up the receiver on the seventh ring.

"You sound out of breath. Did I get you out of the shower?"

The sound of Doris Matthews' voice brought an instant smile. Except for a sympathy card, they hadn't been in touch in over a year. When Doris and her husband lived at the lake, she and Clary had become good friends, thrown together over their mutual concern about Clary's son. Doris had been Richard's ninth grade teacher, and when he started getting bad reports for his behavior and failing his classes, Doris had taken him under her wing. After her divorce, she'd packed up her daughter and moved to San Francisco, where she'd found a new teaching job and resumed her life.

"Actually, I haven't had a decent shower in two weeks," Clary told her. "Since I broke my foot, it's spit baths only."

"Oh honey, I'm so sorry. How'd you do it?"

As Clary related the story, rustling came across the line, and she could picture Doris adjusting the receiver as she painted her nails or primped her hair.

When she finished, Doris said, "I can't imagine dealing with broken bones. Your life must be unbearable."

Clary started to tell her just how unbearable when Doris rushed in with a question.

"Are your cabins booked up now? I'm working on my master's thesis, and I was wondering if Marissa could come stay for a while. An empty house would help my concentration, and it'd be a nice start for her summer vacation. She used to love it at the lake."

Clary tried to recall Doris's daughter and pictured a scrawny kid with a mop of golden hair and a shy smile. That was eight years ago. The child must be in her teens now.

"I'd love to have Marissa," Clary said, "but this broken foot's going to keep me from being much of a surrogate mother.
Besides, the cabins are a mess. I don't know when I'll be able to get them cleaned up."

"Oh hell, Clary. Marissa doesn't need anyone to mother her. She's fifteen years old, for God's sake. And as to the cabins, she's perfectly capable of cleaning her own. It wouldn't hurt her one bit to buckle down and do some work for a change."

Even though she felt reluctant to have a teenager here on her own, Clary thought about the income and decided she couldn't afford to turn Doris down.

They agreed on the rent, and Doris said she'd drive Marissa up the next day. Clary hung up, feeling grateful and relieved. At least she'd be able to keep the wolf from her door a little while longer. The last thing she wanted was to get herself in a position where she might lose this property.

Chapter Two

Clary watched from the window as Doris and Marissa pulled into the yard, their car nosing to a stop beside her truck. Neither of them made a move to get out, and from their head shaking and gesturing, Clary guessed they were having an argument.

Finally, Doris threw open her door with enough force to loosen the hinges, slammed it, and marched toward the house. Clary came out onto the porch, wondering what had upset her so much.

When she saw Clary, Doris smiled tightly and rushed forward with outstretched arms. Her embrace short-circuited when she saw the cast.

"You really did do yourself some damage."

"Enough to keep me from even thinking about jogging for another ten years. You're looking good," Clary said, meaning it.

Doris gave a deprecating shrug. "Sometimes divorce works miracles. I've dropped twelve pounds, had a makeover." She touched her bright red hair. "I even hit the gym a few times a week. Without Donald, life is sweet. God, I don't know why I put up with him as long as I did. Single is the only way to go, right?"

Clary felt her throat constrict and the skin over her cheekbones tighten.

Doris noticed. "Oh, hey, I'm sorry. Me and my big mouth. I heard about Barbara from someone in town. I forget who. Did you get my card? I wanted to come see her, but before I could get it together, she - - - well, you know."

Died, Clary thought. *She died.* Why were people so afraid of the word? Rather than make Doris feel more uncomfortable, she let it go.

"I'm mending," she said simply.

Doris glanced in the direction of the lake.

"What's all the construction over on the south shore? The place is torn up so bad, it looks like a freeway's going in."

"This mogul from Los Angeles, Gerald Kahn, has decided to put up housing for the rich and tasteless. He started buying property last year and building about six months ago. The architecture looks like something straight out of Disneyland, but frankly, I don't care what he does as long as he leaves this side of the lake alone. Barbara was totally against giving him this place, and I have no intentions of parting with it, either."

"I can see why," Doris said. "You're lucky to be living here. I like San Francisco, but I miss the lake a lot." She turned and called down to the car, "Marissa. Come say hello to Ms. Webb."

The girl let a full minute pass before exiting the Volvo. She wore a fashionably tattered pair of jeans and a low-necked blouse, which revealed more cleavage than any fifteen-year-old had a right to. Clary noticed that her hair had been allowed to have its own way, and a mass of blonde curls tangled around her cherubic face. She stood with a fist glued to one hip and eyed Clary warily before sauntering up the hill.

"This is Clary Webb," Doris said. "Maybe you remember her from when we lived in Metcalf."

Marissa shrugged.

Embarrassed by her daughter's rudeness, Doris put in quickly, "Well, I guess we should unload the car."

Clary lagged behind as the girl followed her mother to the car. She stood back to watch as Doris opened the trunk and began hoisting out suitcases. When Doris broke a nail and stopped to examine the damage, Marissa raised her eyes to heaven to show her disdain for her mother's ineptness. Grudgingly, she stepped forward to lift out a makeup case and looked in the direction of the cabins.

"Which one's mine?"

Clary pointed. "The first one. Tahoe."

"How cute. I guess you picked that one because it's closest to your house. Like, that way you can keep an eye on me, right?"

Unsure how to respond, Clary reached in her pocket and pulled out the key. Marissa snatched it from her hand.

"Guess that's my cue to go unpack."

Doris gave her an annoyed look as Marissa hauled out another bag and started down the hill.

"I'll chat with Clary for a minute and come tell you goodbye before I leave, okay?" Doris called.

Marissa shrugged. "Whatever."

In the house, Doris made iced tea for them. She presented Clary's glass like a peace offering and perched on the edge of the sofa, resting her hand on Clary's shoulder. Her tone was calculated to persuade. "Marissa's usually not like this. She's upset at leaving her friends. You know what teenagers are like. She'll get over it."

Clary certainly did know what teenagers were like from having raised Karen and Richard. Past experience told her that if Marissa had come against her will, there'd be rocky times ahead.

"Marissa hasn't exactly been a class act this year," Doris said slowly. "A little defiance, an older boyfriend, you know. This is a good way for her to get back on track. She'll be working at the Lassiter Inn from ten until four every day. I arranged it with Ellen Graham last night. That won't give her much time to get into trouble."

An uneasy feeling crept over Clary. "If she's in the habit of getting into trouble, this isn't going to work out, Doris.
I'm glad to do a favor for you but, with this broken foot, I'm not in very good shape to keep track of an unruly teenager."

Indignation spread over Doris's face. "I guess you've forgotten about Richard and how I worked with him when he was Marissa's age. I didn't leave your son in the lurch when the going got rough. I kept on plugging until he got his act together. Have you forgotten that, Clary?"

How could she forget? At one point, Richard had holed up with a girl in her father's garage and set the place on fire with a cigarette. If it hadn't been for Doris's intervention with the school board, he'd have been expelled. She owed Doris a huge debt of gratitude.

Doris went on in a coaxing tone, "Marissa's not a bad kid, Clary. She's just a little mixed up right now. Spending time here at the lake will do her good. Please give her a chance. It'd mean a lot to me."

How could she refuse?

"Okay, Doris. We'll see how it works out."

Clary hoped with all her might that it would. At this stage of the game, she didn't need any more trouble than she already had.

Chapter Three

Clary watched from the porch as Doris went to tell Marissa goodbye. Doris stayed in the cabin less than a minute and came out hurrying, like a person with an urgent need to be someplace else. The tires of the Volvo kicked dust as she revved it up the drive. Clary guessed that her parting words to her daughter were about cooperation and responsibility. Not exactly music to Marissa's ears. Given what she'd seen of Marissa so far, Clary hoped it was true that teenagers respond better to strangers than to their own parents.

She ate lunch and settled into the novel she was reading, which, she decided, was about as interesting as an outdated Sears catalog. She found herself skipping paragraphs, then whole chapters. It was the only book she hadn't read from her last haul from the library, and now it looked like a lost cause. No telling when she'd be able to replenish her supply.

Just as she was about to abandon the book, Marissa's voice wafted in through the screen. "Anybody home?"

Clary went to the door to find her standing on the porch with an armful of dirty sheets and towels.

"Where do you want these?"

"Machine's back here."

Clary opened the door and led the way. In the laundry room, Marissa looked at the Kenmore as if it were a brand new invention. Gingerly, she stuffed the linens in. Clary pulled the knob for water, resting her crutches against the wall to lift the box of soap off the shelf.

"How'd you do it?" Marissa asked. "Break your leg, I mean."

"It's my foot and I did it bar hopping."

The girl's eyebrows hiked in surprise. "Yeah?"

"Just kidding. I jammed it in a pothole, jogging."

"Yeah, right. I'd swallow bar hopping sooner."

"What, I don't look like a jogger?"

Marissa sniffed.

"Well?"

"Like, jogging's not in character for you."

"You don't know a thing about me. How would you know if jogging's in my character or not?"

"I just don't think so."

She walked away, hips swinging.

Clary set her crutches in motion, anxious to establish a rapport with the girl, to demonstrate her good will. This initial interaction might set the tone for the rest of their time together.

"Why don't you come back later for dinner?" she offered. "Nothing gourmet. Steaks and a salad?"

Marissa turned cold eyes on her. "I hear you're a queer."

Clary felt blood surge up her neck and into her face, and her heart thudded inside her chest. Coming from another lesbian, "queer" was a term of endearment. Coming from this upstart teenager, it was a declaration of war.

She brushed the back of her hand across one cheek to cool her anger. This was simply Marissa's way of riling her into an invitation to leave. If she got it, she'd be able to go home with impunity. The blame would lie solely with Clary. Clary wasn't about to give her the satisfaction.

"Who said I was gay?" she asked in a level tone.

"Everyone in Lake Lassiter and people in Metcalf, too. When I was little, I didn't know what it meant. Now that I do, I don't want anything to do with you."

"Your mother never called me a queer, did she?"

"Not exactly, but I always got the idea she thought you and the woman you lived with were weird. I guess that's why she wanted to be your friend. Mom's a do-gooder, in case you hadn't noticed. She feeds stray cats and volunteers at the food bank. Like, you're just one of her causes."

Clary had known Doris Matthews for more than ten years, and there'd never been any hint that she looked down on Clary.

She decided that when name calling hadn't worked, Marissa had switched to casting doubts about her mother's friendship.

She forced a smile. "I'm not a cause to your mother, Marissa. We've always had a good relationship. Several years ago, she did a big favor for me, and I'd like to repay her by helping you. We both know you can find all kinds of excuses for going home, everything from the heat to feeling uncomfortable around me. Or, you can just decide to make the best of it and have a good time."

Marissa shrugged. "Yeah, well."

"In the meantime, if you have to label me," Clary went on, "try lesbian instead of queer. It sits a little better. Now, what about dinner?"

"Thanks, but no thanks."

Marissa turned to go, making a point, it seemed to Clary, of slamming the screen door on her way out.

* * * *

Around four, Clary heard thumps on the veranda and then a rap on the door. By the time she hoisted out of her chair and swung into the crutches, the rapping had become loud and insistent. She opened the door to find John Munger standing on the porch.

Even though he was her nearest neighbor, Clary had little contact with Munger. Before he retired and moved to the lake, he'd been a farmer in Iowa, and he'd brought his small-town ways and bigoted attitude with him. Clary and Barbara had been at the lake less than a week when Norma Latham at the grocery store had warned them about him.

"The only reason people tolerate John is because he stays to himself," she'd said. "But he's just up the road from you two, and he's made it known he doesn't like you. He's been pretty vocal about the reason, too. You know how bigots are. Steer clear of him if you can. John can be mean."

Luckily, in their thirteen years at the lake, she and Barbara had had few occasions to cross paths with Munger.
They were polite if they passed him on the street and always waved when they saw him in his garden. Other than that, they kept their distance.

Now, he stood before Clary dressed in overalls and boots, his weathered face devoid of expression. What he lacked in height, he made up for in girth. His only distinguishing feature was a pair of craggy eyebrows set at a devilish angle above his bland gray eyes. Clary had often thought that, if he had been a little thinner around the middle, he could have doubled for Jack Nicholson.

"What can I do for you, John?" she asked.
"Came to talk to you."

She motioned him inside, where he scuffed his boots on the braided rug and followed her into the living room. She
sank into the sofa, propping the cast on an ottoman. He remained standing stiffly beside her.

He jerked his head in the direction of the cabins. "New guest's sort of young, ain't she? I didn't see any family."

"Fifteen, and she's here alone. I'm doing a favor for her mother, Doris Matthews. They used to live in Metcalf."

He stroked his chin. "I remember the Matthews. She was a teacher, and he delivered the mail."

Clary nodded. She was anxious for him to state his business and leave. "What brings you?"

He crossed his arms over his broad chest. "I've been approached by that Kahn fellow who's doing all the building over on the south shore. Said he'd be interested in buying my place. Told me to consider what I thought it was worth and he'd be back in a few days to discuss it. I hear tell he's been talking to Ellen and Harry Graham, as well."

There were only three houses on this side of the lake: hers, John Munger's, and the Grahams'. The rest of the land was undeveloped, having been purchased by absentee owners for their retirement. It was common knowledge that Kahn had paid outlandishly high prices for the land on the south shore and would probably be willing to pay them over here, too.
It was only a matter of time before Kahn asked her to sell.

"Are you going to sell?" Clary asked.

"Maybe. I'm nearly seventy years old, and I been thinking it might not be a bad idea for me to move closer to my family. I have a son in Dubuque who'd be glad to have me. With the pretty penny I'd get from here, I wouldn't be a money burden leastaways. I figure Kahn talked to you too, and I wondered what you was asking."

"Mr. Kahn hasn't been around," she said shortly.

"Well, it's a surefire bet he will be. You figure a hundred thousand's too much for me to shoot for?"

Clary hoisted out of her chair and slung into her crutches. "I have no idea what your property's worth, John." She took a step toward the door. "If you'll excuse me, I have things to do."

Munger stayed planted in the same spot, obviously dissatisfied with her response.

"I know your place is worth more than mine, what with the rental cabins, but I just want to get an idea. What'll you ask? Hundred and fifty?"

Clary turned to face him squarely. "My place is not for sale at any price."

He looked at her incredulously. "You got to be out of your mind to pass up all that money. Why wouldn't you take it?"

"I'm afraid that's not your business."

Munger flushed and jutted out his lip as he stomped to the door. Before Clary could catch up to open it for him, he'd made his way out and boarded his truck. She watched from the veranda as he jammed it into gear and roared up the hill and out onto the road.

Unperturbed, Clary stayed on the porch to check her bedraggled Boston ferns. Juggling crutches and a watering can at the same time had proved impossible. She and Barbara had kept the place in perfect condition. Alone now, and incapacitated, she wasn't even capable of dusting the furniture. She was too proud to call on anyone in town for help, and it was a sure bet that Munger wouldn't offer his services. Ditto for Marissa Matthews. She'd just have to grit her teeth and wait until her cast came off. That is, unless she could enlist the services of her son, Richard.

Inside, the telephone rang. Lucy nosed at the screen to be sure she'd heard. In her hurry to reach it, Clary snagged a crutch on the edge of the rug. The crutch clattered to the floor, forcing her to hop to the phone on her good leg.

Richard sounded irritated. "What took you so long?"

"In case you've forgotten, I have a good reason for being slow on my feet these days."

"Oh, yeah. That's right. How's your foot doing, anyhow?"

"It's probably healthier than my plants and the swimming
pool, at this point. I was just thinking about you, wondering if you could take some time off to do some watering for me and clean the pool."

"Sure, Mom. I can't say exactly when, but the first chance I get, okay?

"I'd be grateful."

"You know, people in town have been wondering what made you decide to go jogging in the first place. I said maybe you were going out for the Olympics." He laughed at the little joke, sounding boyish and innocent. "Or, maybe you decided it was time to get yourself in shape and go shopping for a new partner."

The remark surprised her. Acknowledging her lesbianism so openly was a far cry from the way Richard used to react.

"No Olympics and no new relationship," Clary assured him. "I wanted to shed a couple of pounds, and running seemed like a good way to do it. The results weren't quite what I expected."

"That's an understatement, Mom. Listen, why I called, you're not using your pickup these days, are you?"

"No. Why?"

"Could I borrow it?"

"What's wrong with your car?"

"Differential's all crapped up. I'm waiting for parts."

Her old Ford truck was about as useful to her these days
as high-heeled shoes. Still, it represented her independence.

"I need my truck, Richard."

"What for? You can't drive it, not with that hunk of plaster on your gas pedal foot."

"I can't drive my truck right now," Clary told him, "but that doesn't mean I won't need it in time."

"It's only for a few days," he argued. "I'll return it with a full tank."

"Can't Cal give you something to drive? Every time I'm at the garage, he has a slew of vehicles sitting around."

"Yeah, waiting for repairs, which are up to me, which won't get done until I have some wheels."

She felt glad that he took his job seriously. He'd moved out at seventeen and spent the next six years living in a dozen different places, doing a dozen different jobs. He called it "getting it together." Clary called it bumming around. When he'd moved back to the lake, she was gratified that he'd acquired enough experience to land a job at Cal's Garage. She wanted to do anything she could to help him succeed.

"You can have the truck for a week," she relented, "and I'll definitely hold you to your promise to return it with a full tank."

"Thanks, Mom. You don't know how you've saved my butt. I'll come over for it in the morning."

"Just don't make it the crack of dawn. Lugging myself around on these crutches wears me out. I need all the rest I can get."

"No problem. I'll bring a sack of groceries. If we're not too busy at work, I'll stay and clean the pool."

"I'd really appreciate that, Richard."

"Take care, and I'll see you in the morning."

She hung up, counting her blessings for the good person that Richard had become. She could see that he was maturing. She felt she could lean on him, and that was nice to know. Especially now that she no longer had Barbara.

Chapter Four

Clary had finished two cups of coffee by the time Richard rolled into the yard with a blond kid in a beat-up Chevy Lumina. Getting out, he said something, grabbed a sack of groceries out of the back, and shoved the door shut with his foot. The driver pumped the accelerator a couple of times for the fun of it and then sped up the drive.

As Richard started for the house, Marissa came down the steps of her cabin. She'd gathered her hair away from her face and toned down the makeup, but she still wore yesterday's

cleavage-revealing blouse, only this time with a skirt instead of jeans.

Her left hand dangled one of the pillbox purses that seemed to be making a comeback; the right hand clutched

a Baby Ruth. She peeled back the wrapper and sucked on it, smiling at Richard.

As she walked up the drive, he paused to stare before coming into the house.

"Who's the babe?"

"Marissa Matthews. You might remember her mother, Doris Matthews."

"Mrs. Matthews, my old teacher?"

"Yes."

He set the groceries on the counter, pulling out a sack of chips and diving in for a handful. "The daughter looks like trouble."

Clary observed that, even at twenty-three, Richard looked much the same as he had as a teenager, the same unruly yellow hair swooping in wings to his eyebrows, the same pale complexion, the beautiful dark lashes fringing mahogany eyes. He had his father's coloring.

"Marissa's staying for the summer and working over at the Inn part time," she told him.

"Good luck." He took another fistful of chips from the bag and stuffed them in his mouth. "Ellen Graham will run her ragged. And with those looks, the Graham Cracker'll have the kid serving drinks in no time. Who's to stop her? Harry Graham, our beloved chief of police?"

Clary hoped he was wrong. She'd be less than thrilled at having to tell Doris that her underage daughter was dispensing booze at the local watering hole.

She noticed Richard looking down at her cast. "It's a thing of beauty, isn't it?" she commented.

"To an orthopedist, I guess. How long does it have to stay on?"

"Too long." She moved to the key rack, retrieving the set to her truck. "Enjoy," she said, dropping the keys into his hand.

He stuffed them in his pocket and bent to peck her on the cheek. "Thanks, Mom." He checked his watch. "I told Cal I'd be a little late so I could work on the pool. I don't know why you don't fill it up with sand. No one uses it anymore."

"I use it, or at least I did before I botched up my foot."

Richard shrugged. "Whatever. It'll take me about an hour. Then, I'll water your plants."

"Wonderful. Oh, if you don't see me around when you're finished, it's probably because I've gone to take a nap. We invalids are allowed to do that, you know."

"Lucky you."

At the door, she asked, "Is everything going okay? Getting enough to eat, keeping ahead of the laundry?"

"Believe it or not, I do pretty well on my own. Better than you, for sure. Give me a call if I can give you a lift to the doctor or anything."

"Thank you, Richard."

With Richard out the door, she thought about brewing another pot of coffee to keep herself going, then discarded the idea. What difference did it make if she went back to bed? She certainly didn't intend to weed the garden or clean the house today.

Yawning, she meandered to the bedroom, drew the blinds, and lay down on the bed. She was quickly asleep.

She might have slept for hours except for the phone ringing. Resisting the impulse to rush to answer, she decided to let whoever it was leave a message.

Lying on her back, she listened to the muffled voice on the tape before the machine clicked off. It was a woman's voice, but she couldn't place it. Curious, she got up and changed her shirt, damp from lying in one place in the hot room. Lucy, who'd stretched herself full length on the coolness of the wooden floor, got to her feet as Clary maneuvered into her crutches. Her tail swung happily as she followed to the kitchen.

Even though it felt longer, the wall clock said she'd dozed less than two hours. Groggily, she rewound the answering machine and punched it to play back.

"Clary, this is Jo. You've probably forgotten my voice." An embarrassed laugh followed. "My vacation started yesterday. No more squinting at doctor's hieroglyphics in that stuffy pharmacy for a while. I long for the sight of trees and a swim in the lake. If you have room for me, I'd like to come up and spend a few days unwinding. Call me, okay?" She ended with her number.

Wide awake now, Clary picked up the receiver and dialed Jo's number. Jo answered on the second ring, sounding surprised by the quick response.

"That was speedy. You must be monitoring your messages," she said.

"Actually, I was asleep."

"Oh, I'm sorry. If this is a bad time for you, I can call back."

"No, it's okay," Clary cut in. "I'd love to have you come up. I'm not booked, and the last time I looked, the lake was still there. I haven't seen it up close for a couple of weeks though. Broke my foot."

"Oh no. Kick the TV set or what?" Jo laughed.

"I was jogging to lose weight and met up with a pothole. I'm pretty much a couch potato and absolutely useless when it comes to cleaning. You'll have to be your own maid."

"That's no problem. When would be a good time for me to come?"

"Today, if you like," Clary said.

"Maybe we could have lunch when I get there. It'd give us a chance to catch up."

"We certainly have plenty of that to do," Clary agreed.

"I'll see you soon, then."

* * *

As Clary struggled with the lid on a new jar of mayonnaise, she remembered when Jo had started coming to the lake. Was it ten or eleven years ago? Jo had met Barbara at a book signing in San Francisco and found that she liked the author as well as she liked her novels. They'd had coffee afterward and discovered that they had more in common than Barbara's work. After that, Jo came for a stay every time she got the chance, on weekends and on her vacations from the hospital, where she worked as a pharmacist. Sometimes she'd bring a friend, a woman she'd met at work or at her book club. All of them were attractive, but the attachments never seemed to last, and most of the time Jo came by herself.

On those occasions, Barbara and Clary often invited her to the house in the evenings. The three of them would play cards, cook, watch movies. Jo was the youngest of the three, and she jokingly called Barbara "Mom" and pretended that she and Clary were sisters.

Clary remembered a Saturday night about three years ago, long before Barbara's illness had begun to incapacitate her, when the three of them were making spaghetti and meatballs. Clary had elected to chop the onions, and halfway through, she had rivers of tears streaming down her cheeks.

Jo had crossed the kitchen and put her arms around her waist. "Don't cry, Sis," she had teased. "You may have to take some antacid afterward, but the spaghetti won't be so bad that you'll end up in the emergency room."

Playfully, Clary had pushed her away. "Our spaghetti is wonderful, and you know it. It's these damned onions."

"Poor baby," Barbara put in from the stove, where she stood tending the sauce. "Want to trade jobs with me?"

"No need for that," Jo said. "We'll just pull the old bread-in-the-mouth trick." She crossed to the refrigerator, took out a slice of bread, and handed it to Clary. "Here. Clamp your teeth down on this. It will absorb the fumes and stop you from blubbering."

Clary put the bread in her mouth and continued chopping. She wasn't aware that Jo and Barbara had been staring at her until they both broke out in gales of laughter.

She snatched the bread out of her mouth. "What's so funny?"

Barbara made her face a blank. "Nothing, honey. You just looked a little . . ."

"Stupid," Jo said through her uproarious laughter. "That piece of bread hanging out of your face like a big, white tongue."

"Well, it was your idea, Jo. If I looked stupid, it was your fault."

"I was only trying to help," Jo retorted.

"You knew it'd look stupid before you suggested it."

Barbara plunked her spoon down loudly on the stove. "That's enough, children. Now, get back to work so we can have some dinner."

"Yes, Mother," Jo and Clary chorused, and all three of them had laughed.

After dinner, they watched a video Jo had rented from a women's bookstore. It was titled *Desire* and appropriately so. As they watched two scantily clad women cavorting in a spa, Barbara moved closer to Clary on the sofa and stroked the back of her neck. A surge of warmth spread to her face and trickled down her spine. A sigh escaped her lips and Jo, who was sitting on the floor, turned around.

"Hot stuff, eh?" she asked.

"Very," Barbara answered.

Jo kept her eyes on them for a minute, a knowing smile on her lips. She turned back to the video as Barbara's hand slid down to caress Clary's shoulders. Clary sighed again, but this time it was as much because she felt sorry about Jo's solitary situation as it was from arousal.

Later, as they lay nestled in one another's arms in bed, Barbara had whispered in Clary's ear, "What did you think of the babes in the video?"

"Like Jo said, hot stuff."

Barbara moved her mouth closer to Clary's ear.

"Definitely hot." She prolonged the *F* sound, sending out a stream of warm air. Clary shivered. Barbara reached with an index finger and traced small circles on Clary's forehead. "And which of the hot babes turned you on the most?"

"The blonde who kept escaping to her bedroom to write in her journal."

Barbara's fingers slid over Clary's temples and cheeks, settling at her mouth, where they continued their trip around her lips. "I thought you might favor that one."

Clary teased the tip of Barbara's finger with her tongue, then took it inside her mouth. "Why did you think that?" She spoke around the fingertip.

"You like blondes, that's why. You picked me, didn't you?"

"I think it was the other way around, darling. You picked me." She stopped to kiss the palm of Barbara's hand. "For which, I shall forever be grateful."

Barbara shifted her weight, nudging Clary's thigh with a knee and resting her hand on one breast. "Even if my hair is turning to gray?"

"Even if it turns snow white. Which girl did you like best?"

"Guess."

"The redhead with the big boobs and the nipples that stood up like grapes."

"Ready for the squeezing? Like this?" Gently, she took Clary's nipple between her thumb and index finger and played with it.

"Yes, like that."

Barbara released the nipple and smoothed her fingers over the fullness of Clary's breast. "You have wonderful breasts. Every bit as nice as the redhead's." She nuzzled Clary's ear again. "I love your breasts."

Clary reached out to reciprocate the wonderful stroking, which was prompting the old, familiar feeling of wetness and heaviness between her legs. From the first time they had made love, it had taken only minutes for Barbara to put her in a state of complete surrender. Clary raised up on an elbow, keeping her hand cupped around Barbara's small breast, and kissed her.

"Touch me," she said. Touch me until I fly to heaven."

Sliding her hands down Clary's belly, Barbara complied. "Oh, my," she said, "I don't think your trip will take long at all."

* * * *

Jo arrived around one, and they settled down to a lunch of egg salad sandwiches and small talk in the airy living room. Clary admired Jo's new haircut and described how it felt trying to manage with a broken foot. Jo told of wallpapering her kitchen and starting an herb garden. They exchanged details of the books they'd read and the films they'd seen. It took them a long time to get around to Barbara.

"I was glad you could make it to the funeral," Clary said quietly. "Barbara was so observant, being a writer, you know, that I'm sure she was looking down and making notes about who came and who didn't."

Jo rewarded the humor with a weak smile. Then she pulled in a long breath and stared at her feet. When she raised her head to look at Clary, her hazel eyes had filled with pain. "Barbara was very dear to me. It would have taken an earthquake, or worse, to keep me away."

Clary said, "It was a nice service, wasn't it? Plain, the way Barbara wanted it. I was surprised at how many people showed up. We weren't exactly the town's favorite couple, you know. They really came for the Hadley family, not for Barbara. Certainly not for me." She smiled. "When I got home, someone had left a bottle of bourbon on the porch. No note, just the booze. I've often wondered who. And why."

Jo said nothing. An awkward silence followed as the two women tried to keep their emotions in check. Clary found a piece of eggshell in her sandwich. She picked it out and put it on the side of her plate. A fly buzzed against the screen. The heavy fragrance of jasmine drifted through an open window. Lucy scratched at her ear.

After a while, Jo said, "I'm sorry I wasn't able to visit more often while Barbara was sick. I know that she would have liked to see me, and you probably could have used the moral support. My work schedule isn't always . . . " She broke off, unable to finish.

Quickly Clary said, "The flowers you sent were great. Barbara loved carnations. We couldn't grow them here, not the right kind of soil."

"I'm glad. I wanted you to know I was thinking of you two." Her thoughts were interrupted suddenly, and she stared at Clary with concern. "Are you okay, Clary? I know it's only been six months, but you really don't look well."

Clary shrugged it off. "It'll take a while for me to recuperate. It's been a horrible time. I'm sure you can imagine. I was barely starting to get over Barbara's death when I was slapped with the reality of my situation. Broken foot, no job, cabins empty. Things are pretty tough, especially tough now that I can't work."

"What about the royalties from her books?"

"She didn't exactly write bestsellers. The small presses that published her books don't have a huge following. I get a check every four months, but so far, they don't even put groceries on the table. Frankly, I don't know how I'm going to manage until I can get back to work or find a way to fill the cabins for the summer." She laughed to lighten the atmosphere. "Let's just say, I don't indulge in filet mignon and champagne any more."

"I know you love it here, but what about selling this

place and moving to a city where you could get a job?" Jo suggested.

Clary shook her head as she ran her fingers through the short-cropped hair she cut herself now. "Definitely not. The cabins put food on the table. I plan to stay in my home, our home, Barbara's and mine, until the day I die."

"Well," Jo said, standing up. "You said you had cabins to clean?"

"Your old Telluride is really a mess. I warned you."

"So you did. Walk down with me, and I'll get started."

As they stepped off the porch, Marissa came down the drive, her arms encircling two grocery bags.

"Been shopping?" Clary asked when they came close.

"What's it look like? I even got broccoli. That'd make my mother proud."

"Marissa, this is my friend Jo Taylor. She'll be staying in the other cabin."

Marissa took Jo in with a sweeping glance before focusing pointedly on Clary. "At least you have good taste."

The implication was that they were more than friends.

When she and Jo had moved a few feet away, Marissa called, "By the way, I have a bulletin. If you don't clean my stove, there's liable to be a fire. Like, the bottom of that oven looks like two years of baked-on crud."

Clary called back, "You have two choices. You can either clean the stove yourself or stick to Baby Ruths and raw broccoli until I get around with the Oven Off."

Marissa shrugged. "It's up to you. I'd hate to see this place go up in smoke."

Walking to the cabin, Jo asked, "What's with Miss Congeniality?"

"She's the daughter of a friend. I owe her mother a favor and having the girl here is it."

"If you ask me, you don't need more trouble at this point," Jo said.

Clary knew she was right. She only hoped that her relationship with Marissa didn't get any worse.

Chapter Five

Having your foot in a cast, Clary decided, prompted you to consider things that had never occurred to you before. For example, did people who broke one foot have to replace their shoes because of the one worn member of each pair? What age was the cut-off for having friends autograph a cast? And, should she convert the pants with only one leg into shorts, or simply relegate them to the trash?

She pondered this trivia as she got dressed on the morning after Jo's arrival. As she slid into a pair of shorts, she heard the slam of Tahoe's door and looked out in time to see Marissa setting off for work. Before turning away from the window, she caught herself staring at Jo's cabin. Jo's car was parked outside and the window shades were drawn. On this first day of her vacation, she was probably sleeping in.

As Clary turned away from the window to make herself some breakfast, she found herself wondering how much she and Jo would see of one another. She hadn't realized how lonely she'd been. Karen, her daughter, lived over three hundred miles away in San Francisco, and Richard's job kept him tethered to the garage. She was friendly with Norma Latham down at the grocery store, but most of the lake people were only minimally polite. She knew that Jo had come primarily to rest and relax, but she hoped her old friend would want to spend time with her. Friendships such as Jo's were valuable, especially since Jo had known Barbara and had a part in their mutual history.

After breakfast, Clary rambled around the house, haphazardly straightening up as best she could on her crutches. The day loomed before her, long and empty. She disliked TV, and she'd run out of reading material, so she decided to take her pad and some pencils and go outside to sketch.

Before her accident, she'd taken up oil painting and had become so good that, when Norma had displayed some of her paintings in the store, people had offered to buy them. Clary had entertained the idea of selling her work on a full-time basis. Now the idea seemed more appealing than ever. Even after she went back to work at the hardware store, the extra money would come in handy.

She shut Lucy in the house and hauled her materials to the road, where she settled on a tree stump and began to work. The sun infused her back and arms with warmth, and soon she was lost in concentration as she labored to reproduce a patch of wild lavender.

She was startled by the sound of a car coming fast down her side of the road, and she looked up to see a red Lincoln Towncar pull to a stop on the berm. She'd seen the car in town before. It belonged to Gerald Kahn.

The driver's window whined down, and Carl Smail's broad face appeared against a backdrop of crimson leather. His skin was the color of coffee laced with cream, and he sported a single gold loop in one ear. No one seemed quite sure about Smail's connection to Kahn. Some said chauffeur, some said bodyguard. Whatever his function, he was never more than an arm's length away from the wealthy developer.

Smail propped a muscled arm on the ledge and pushed his face into the sunlight through the open window. His shaved head gleamed, as if he'd slathered it with oil.

"You got a minute? Mr. Kahn wants to speak to you."

Clary realized that Kahn must be sitting in the back, hidden from view by the tinted windows and that, sitting on her tree stump with a pencil in her hand, she had no excuse to refuse. She'd expected him to approach her about her property sooner or later, and now was probably as good a time as any for her to deal with him.

She'd barely nodded her permission when the back door of the vehicle swung open, and Gerald Kahn climbed out. He was built like a tree trunk, more or less, and his face carried an expression of guarded suspicion. His large pointed nose and the way his jowls overlapped his collar gave him the appearance of a turtle and, even though he probably had it professionally styled, his hair bushed out wildly as if it had never made the acquaintance of styling gel or a comb. Without smiling, he stepped carefully through the weeds to where she was sitting and extended a beefy hand.

"I'm Gerald Kahn, Mrs. Ingersoll." He hesitated for a second. "Or is it Miss Webb?"

Clary hadn't gone by her married name in years. In fact, she doubted that anyone in Lake Lassiter even knew what it was. It seemed obvious that Kahn had taken pains to research her background.

She shook his hand briefly, pulling back at the touch of soft flesh bathed in sweat.

"It's Ms. Webb. Capital m, small s, period. I took back my maiden name some time ago, in the interest of pursuing my freedom."

A slight smile curled his thick lips. "Yes. Your neighbors apprised me of your pursuit of freedom, as you call it." He gestured at the surroundings. "This isn't the ideal place for us to talk. I tried your house first. It was just luck that Carl spotted you sitting here."

"What can I do for you, Mr. Kahn?"

He shoved his hands into his trouser pockets and fixed his gaze on her. "I'd like to talk to you about your property."

"You'd like to buy it," she said, picking up her pencil.

"How did you know?"

"Everyone in Lake Lassiter knows you're the man who bought up the south shore and started building there. When my neighbor John Munger told me that you'd come to him, it just stood to reason that you've decided to develop this side of the lake, too."

Kahn nodded. "So, that out of the way, are you interested in selling to me?"

"No, I'm not." She debated whether to leave it at that or to explain. Chances were that he'd ask her for a reason, so she decided to get it out of the way. "I never had a real home growing up. I spent my childhood in foster homes. When I moved here with my partner, I felt as if I'd finally found a home. I don't ever intend to sell it. I'm sorry, Mr. Kahn."

She looked up to see him chewing on his bottom lip, a look of consternation on his face. He failed to reply for a few seconds.

"I'm sorry, too, Ms. Webb. I grew up in the country, and I can appreciate how you feel about this lake. It's definitely peaceful and pleasant here. But, in light of your recent loss, I thought you might be ready to make a change. When our circumstances change, our feelings about things sometimes change, too."

She wondered who'd told him. John Munger, or maybe Ellen Graham. Lake Lassiter was basically a goldfish bowl, so it might have been anyone.

"If anything, my loss has made me feel even more attached to the lake," she replied.

The look of consternation on Kahn's face increased. Suddenly, he jutted out his hand, palm up, as if testing for rain, and Carl jumped out of the car and produced a cigar, plucking a lighter from his pocket. He stood at least six foot four, and the muscles in his arms tightened as he touched the end of the cigar with the flame. He watched his boss puff on it and, when he was sure it was underway, he got back in the car.

Kahn cleared his throat. "Ms. Webb, I am prepared to offer you a great deal of money for your place, much more I'm sure than you could ever hope to get from anyone else. Your house and those rundown cabins are worth nothing to me, of course. I am interested only in the land."

"It's irrelevant to me whether you want the land, the buildings or both. And it doesn't matter how much you are prepared to offer. I am not interested in selling." Clary bent her head and began shading in the leaves of a lavender plant. She heard the scrunch of Kahn's expensive shoes on the gravel as he paced. She kept sketching.

He came to a halt in front of her, his words measured and deliberate. "It's not my habit to discuss price until I have a verbal agreement to sell, but in this case I'll make an exception. I will give you two hundred thousand dollars. That's roughly three times the market value. Surely, that much money is enough to make you reconsider."

In spite of herself, Clary felt her heart accelerate. Two years ago, a realtor from Metcalf had come by to make an offer on behalf of a vacationing couple who'd seen her property from the road and wanted a place for the summers. His offer had been fifty thousand, a quarter of Kahn's offer. With two hundred thousand dollars, she could pay off her debts and have enough left over to live very comfortably. Although she hated to admit it, even to herself, the offer was enticing.

She looked down toward the lake, shimmering aquamarine under the clear sky, and she remembered the morning six months ago when she had risen at dawn to scatter Barbara's ashes along the shoreline. Barbara had stipulated it in her will and had felt so strongly about it that, from her hospital bed, she'd made Clary promise, again.

"I want you to scatter my remains along the lake where we spent so many good times together," she'd said. "Don't let anyone talk you into a plot someplace. The happiest times of my life have been spent here with you, and I want to spend my eternity here, too."

Clary pulled herself back into the present and realized that Kahn was looking at her for an answer.

"Your offer is generous, but I'm afraid that money is not the issue. I stand by my refusal."

Kahn sucked in his breath, and Clary was struck by the way his cheeks reddened and his eyes bulged as he listened to her words. It was clear that he was used to getting his way and, now, when he couldn't, he was visibly affected.

He turned away, puffing furiously on the cigar, and when he turned back, Clary felt alarm at the fury in his eyes.

"Ms. Webb," he sputtered, "as you probably know, I have approached several of your neighbors about selling and have been met with willingness, if not downright gratitude. To a soul, people are anxious to move away from this hick town and do it with enough money to start the kind of life they've always dreamed about. Unlike you, they recognize a once-in-a-lifetime opportunity when they see it."

Clary shrugged. "That's up to them."

"That's not exactly true, and you know it."

"What do you mean?"

"The damned access road is what I mean," he stormed. "You've played your little game long enough. Why don't you just lay your cards on the table and let's get this thing over with!"

Clary felt totally lost. It must have showed on her face because Kahn cocked his head for an instant and frowned before saying, "Don't insult my intelligence by trying to tell me that you don't know about the access road, the one that forks off at the far end of your property."

Still befuddled, Clary shook her head.

Kahn swung his large head from side to side, breathing rapidly, and Clary wasn't sure who he was the more angry with, himself or her.

"I can't believe that you don't know about it. It's on your property, goddamn it. You own it."

Clary felt her jaw slacken as she processed the information. Barbara had never mentioned the road. Perhaps she hadn't realized that it was part of her land. In the whole time they'd lived there, nothing had ever occurred to make them aware of it. The road hadn't meant a thing to them. What it meant to Gerald Kahn was that he couldn't transport one sackful of nails or one truckload of lumber to the lakeshore without owning the access road, which belonged to her.

Clary resisted the urge to smile as she looked at Kahn.

"I can see how the access road will interfere with your plans," she said, "but I'm afraid I don't have enough sympathy for you to change my mind. My decision is irrevocable."

Kahn swung his head and emitted a tortured sound as he flung his cigar into the dirt and ground it to pulp with the toe of his polished shoe.

"Well, I can tell you this, your neighbors aren't going to be thrilled with your irrevocable decision. From what I hear, some of them haven't been exactly thrilled with you as a neighbor from the beginning. In a small town like this, people share things, and more than a handful have shared their feelings about you. Ms. Hadley grew up here, and so she was more or less accepted, gay or not. Now that she's no longer in the picture, I wouldn't be surprised if you got flack. Not only are you a lesbian, but your refusing to sell to me puts a monkey wrench in their plans. I wouldn't be surprised if you got a lot of flack."

Clary felt hot rage come to life as her heart whammed in her chest. Without thinking, she grabbed her crutch and started to stand, with every intention, she realized suddenly, of bludgeoning Kahn with it. The only thing that kept her from it was losing her balance. Breathing hard, she fell back onto the tree stump and sat there shaking while she fought to gain control of herself.

It took her a minute to rcover her senses and force reason to take over. Let Gerald Kahn try to intimidate her with all the homophobic remarks in the world. It was he who should be on the defensive, not her. She needed to remember that.

With a great deal of effort, she finally relaxed her muscles and eased her tortured breathing. She looked Kahn in the eye.

"I'm well aware that some of my neighbors don't like me," she said.

"A few of them, John Munger, for example, have made no bones about it, and I'm sure there are others who hide their hatred simply to keep the peace. If my refusal to sell my property causes them to give me flack, so be it. As a gay woman, I've experienced a lot of flack in my life. I think I can handle it."

Kahn opened his mouth to reply but clamped it shut immediately, probably realizing that there was nothing he could say to change her mind. He simply looked at her and turned in resignation for his car.

As soon as he shut the door, Smail revved up the engine, then allowed it to idle while he tried to determine if Kahn was finished or not.

Kahn rolled down his window and called out, "If you change your mind, let me know. Anyone in town can tell you where to find me."

"I'll do that," she said shortly.

The window went up again, and Smail eased the car onto the road, the sound of the engine barely ruffling the air as he drove off.

Clary spent the next few minutes working on her sketch, but her enthusiasm had dulled. Listlessly, she closed her sketch pad and tucked the pencils in her pocket.

Going back to the house, she wondered if she'd seen the last of Kahn. Somehow, she doubted it.

Chapter Six

Even though Kahn held no sway over Clary, their confrontation left her feeling depressed. His anger when she'd refused to sell to him was frightening and, in spite of herself, she felt threatened. Without admitting to herself why she was doing it, she took extra pains for the next couple of days to make sure the doors and windows were locked at night.

Awakened one morning by the loud music coming from Marissa's cabin, she hauled herself out of bed, determined to erase all thoughts of Kahn from her mind. She downed a bowl of cereal, bathed as much as possible with the cast, and ventured onto the veranda.

It was early and yet jet skiers and swimmers peppered the lake. Before summer ended, the population of Lassiter would double with tourists. They polluted the lake with trash, made parking a nightmare, crowded the restaurants, and wreaked havoc in bars. But the town needed their dollars. Without them, Lake Lassiter would be every bit as prosperous as a ghost town.

Ghost town. The words echoed in her head, and she remembered her impression of Lake Lassiter the first time Barbara had brought her and the children to see it. It had been a chill October day with a cold wind gusting dust and scraps of trash down the street. Not a soul in sight. They'd driven slowly through town, and Barbara had played tour guide, as excited as only a person who'd grown up here could be.

"There's Latham's Grocery," she said pointing, "and over there is Dave's Shoe Repair. He takes forever to get anything done, but the price is right. Down the block is Cal's Garage. You'll gas up there, no other tanks this side of Metcalf. The library is right across the street, and next door is Ernie's Short Cut. Cutsie name for a barbershop, but Ernie does good work."

"Is there a beauty shop?" Clary asked.

Barbara turned to her and reached to ruffle her straight, dark hair. "What do you care? It's not as if you need to touch up your roots and get a pedicure every week."

"Just wondering."

From the back seat, where he'd been racing toy cars up and down the rear window, ten-year-old Richard piped up, "Where's the mall? Do they have a video arcade?"

"My dear boy," Barbara said, "after we move here, you're going to find lots of things to do beside waste your money on video machines."

"Like what?"

"Like fish in the lake, plant a garden, learn to row a boat."

"I don't like any of that stuff."

Clary opened her mouth to remind Richard of his manners, but before she could, Barbara said firmly, "You will learn to love that stuff, trust me."

Clary turned briefly to see Richard's downcast eyes and pouting mouth. He looked up momentarily to see if she would back him up, and when she didn't, he turned back to playing Indie 500 with his cars, happy as ever.

She smiled over at Barbara, a silent thank you for the discipline that Richard had been missing since his father left. She tried to make the children behave, but all too often she let things slide. She felt grateful that Barbara had chosen to take an active part in the children's lives, feeling as free to guide them as to love them.

Throughout the trip, Karen had occupied herself with her paper doll Barbies, appearing not to take any interest in the conversation. Now she said, "We don't have to fish, do we? I don't want to kill any fish. I like to go to the movies, that's what I want to do."

"Me too," Clary said. Then to Barbara, "Where's the local Bijou?"

"On the corner of fifth and Main in Metcalf."

"Twenty miles away?"

"Afraid so. But we get TV here at the lake."

"Black and white, four whole channels," Clary replied with sarcasm.

Barbara patted Clary's leg. "Color and five channels. You'll survive. You like to read, and the library's well stocked, as far as small town libraries go. And now that I can work at home, slaving away at the Great American Novel, we can spend more time together. The kids will be at school all day and . . . " She broke off and cocked her head toward the back seat. "We'll find plenty to do."

Clary knew what she had in mind. And the idea kicked her heart beat into third gear.

Now, hobbling around the broad porch, Clary inspected her plants and gingerly made her way into the yard. Patches of tinder-dry weeds had taken over the area all the way from her house to the shoreline, and she worried once again about the threat of fire. One of these days she was going to have to get Richard to cut them down.

She could see Jo, stretched out in a deck chair under the eaves of her cabin, a book in hand. Since Jo had moved in, Clary had only spotted her once or twice from her window, coming and going to the lake. Now, Jo looked up from her book and motioned to her. Clary maneuvered over the uneven ground down to the cabin.

Jo plucked off her sunglasses and perched them atop her head as Clary came alongside the porch.

"Where've you been, stranger?" she asked.

"Holed up inside, counting the roses on the wallpaper, I'm afraid. Richard borrowed my truck, so I couldn't go anywhere even if I could drive. Besides that, something happened a couple of days ago that turned me into a nervous wreck."

"What's that?"

Clary told her about the meeting with Kahn, ending with "Frankly, the guy makes my skin crawl. Lord knows I could use two hundred thousand dollars right now, but even if I did want to sell my property, it wouldn't be to him. I'd rather see the devil himself get this place. Not that it matters.
I have every intention of spending the rest of my days right here the way Barbara and I would have, if she'd lived."

Jo reserved comment and stared off toward the lake, lost in thought. Clary interpreted this as a signal that she wantd to be left alone. But when she turned to leave, Jo suddenly looked up.

"By the way, how are you fixed for groceries these days?"

The change of subject surprised Clary. "Not great. With this foot and no transportation, getting to the store is impossible."

"That's what I figured. I don't plan to go for a swim until later. Why don't I ferry you over to Latham's grocery, then on the way back we can stop for a couple of those wonderful hamburgers at the Lassiter Inn. Ellen still serves them, doesn't she?"

As far as Clary knew, she did, accompanied by ample servings of derision and rudeness. Most of Lassiter had eventually come to accept Barbara and Clary, but not Ellen Graham. At every opportunity, she went out of her way to belittle their relationship.

Clary remembered one January night five years ago when she and Barbara had stopped at the Inn. It had

been freezing cold, and dinner in front of the fireplace had lured them
inside. Barbara, who watched her weight meticulously, had ordered a Caesar salad, Clary a bowl of clam chowder. As the waitress made for the kitchen, Ellen stopped her, took their order slip, and sauntered over to their table. People at nearby tables stopped eating to witness the lesbian-baiting that they knew was coming.

"Evening, ladies," Ellen crooned, placing an unmistakable emphasis on the "ladies." "In case you didn't know, every Thursday is couple's night, and tonight we have a sirloin special. You're definitely some sort of a couple." She raised a penciled eyebrow. "Why not try it?"

She smiled around at the other diners. On purpose, no one noticed.

Instantly, Clary bristled. "Yes, we are a couple. Was it Barbara's combat boots or my tattoos that tipped you off?"

Barbara, who hated unpleasantness, shook her head at Clary in admonishment.

"We'll stick to our first choice," she said quietly. "Maybe we'll get the special next time."

There hadn't been a next time. They'd avoided the Lassiter Inn from then on.

Clary told the story to Jo in the car, her heart racing as she relived it.

"That was a long time ago," Jo said. "Times change, people change. Surely, you're not still holding a grudge."

"No grudge," Clary defended. "It just left a bad taste in my mouth, which I'm not anxious to experience again."

"I wouldn't worry. I know people who wouldn't give me the time of day five years ago. Now I'm the token lesbian at their parties."

Clary doubted that Ellen would welcome her to the Inn, even as a token. In deference to Jo, however, she agreed to go.

After picking up groceries, they drove to the Inn and went inside. It was barely eleven thirty, too early for the lunch crowd, and, except for the coffee drinkers who habitually held sway over the counter seats, the place was empty.

After she and Jo settled at a window table, Clary looked around for Ellen and Marissa, but neither were in sight. She was just beginning to relax when Ellen swished through the swinging door from the kitchen, wielding a coffeepot. She looked as though she'd applied her makeup with a trowel, and her hoop earrings swung against her cheeks as she bantered back and forth with the men at the counter. Quickly, Clary turned her face to the window, hoping that Ellen wouldn't spot her, but a minute later she appeared at their table with her order pad.

"Clary?" she said, barely acknowledging her. Then to Jo, "We haven't seen you in a long time."

"I just came up for a few days to get away from the city and enjoy a change of scenery. I'm staying in one of Clary's cabins."

Ellen nodded curtly. "What can I get you?"

"I thought Marissa might be our waitress," Clary put in.

"She's staying at my place, too."

"So she tells me. She's been out all morning running errands. Nice to have an extra pair of hands, what with the tourists. Soup of the day is potato, by the way."

They both ordered hamburgers, fries, and cokes, dawdling over their food to enjoy the view of the lake. Not much conversation passed between them, and Clary felt relieved not to have the burden of making small talk. She was comfortable just sitting here with Jo, even though being close to such an attractive woman made her miss Barbara even more.

Will the day ever come when I stop remembering, stop thinking of Barbara? Clary thought. Will there come a time when I can turn down the bed and not hesitate because I'm waiting for Barbara? A morning I can make coffee without taking two cups out of the cupboard? When I can catch the fragrance of her perfume in a dresser drawer and not be blinded by tears? Until the end of her life, she doubted that such a day would ever come.

When she and Jo had finished their meal, Ellen came back across the room and stood beside the table to total up their check. Without meeting Clary's eyes, she said, "Has Mr. Kahn been around to see you yet?"

"As a matter of fact, yes, just the other day."

"And?"

"And, although his offer was generous, I'm not going to sell to him."

Ellen stopped writing and looked at Clary sharply. "Why not?"

Clary met her gaze. "Not that it's any of your affair, Ellen, but I simply have no reason to sell."

Ellen's eyes bored into Clary's for a moment before she went back to her order pad. Her face reddened to match her lipstick, and it was easy to see that she was reining in her temper. Finally, unable to contain herself any longer, she demanded, "What's the real problem? Money not enough to satisfy you?"

"As I said, it's really none of your affair."

She knew she was being evasive, but with the way Ellen had treated her and Barbara over the years, she didn't owe the woman a thing.

Ellen remained silent while she finished the check. She started to put it on the table, then changed her mind. "Mind if I sit down?"

The request took Clary off guard, and she wondered what more Ellen could possibly have to say.

She shrugged. "Sure, sit down."

As Ellen pulled out a chair and lowered herself onto it, Jo got out of hers. "I think I'll go outside and get some fresh air while the two of you talk."

"I won't be long," Clary said.

She watched Jo cross the room, then turned her attention to Ellen. In the last few years, Clary had only seen her in the street a few times, not enough to really notice her appearance. Now, she saw that Ellen had bleached her brown hair silvery blonde. If she thought the change subtracted from her age, she was mistaken.

"Decide somewhere along the way it isn't contagious?" Clary asked.

"What isn't?"

"My lesbianism."

Ellen opened her mouth with a comeback, then thought better of it. She pressed her lips into a thin line as she looked out the window. Then, she took a deep breath and looked at Clary.

"You and I have had our differences," she began. "You don't understand my way of life, and I sure as hell don't understand yours. But no matter what we think of each other, we need to talk about this."

Clary watched her warily and twisted her wedding ring on her finger. Lately, she'd caught herself playing with the ring when she felt uncertain and needed confidence. Just touching it seemed to make her feel better.

Barbara had bought twin gold bands for them on a trip to San Francisco shortly after they moved to the lake, and they had exchanged the rings, along with their vows, at lakeside one evening. The vows had been as simple as the rings: promises of everlasting trust, caring, and love. Barbara's ring was still on her hand the day she died, and Clary felt sure that the same would be true for her.

Ellen cleared her throat and scooted closer to the table, folding her hands in front of her on the placemat.

"I've been managing this place for nearly sixteen years, standing on my feet all day and half the night. I'm getting varicose veins on my varicose veins. I'm tired, and Harry's bored. Being chief of police in a place like this just makes him a big fish in a small pond. They've been after him over in Metcalf to come to work. Decent hours, better salary. I could quit working."

She stopped, her eyes searching Clary's face under an awning of mascara. "You see what I'm getting at, don't you?"

Clary did, but she didn't want to give Ellen the satisfaction of admitting it.

She stirred more sugar into her tea. "Tell me."

Ellen batted a strand of platinum hair off her forehead. "We'd like to move to Metcalf, dammit, Clary."

Her outburst made the customers at the counter turn and look. Silence hung like fog over the restaurant. Ellen turned her face to the window to avoid the inquisitive looks of the diners.

"We'd like to sell our place and move to Metcalf," she repeated quietly.

"Then why don't you?"

Ellen spoke through clenched teeth. "You know good and well why we can't. Kahn made you a very decent offer. He wants your place and the access road as much as Harry and I want him to have it. Why won't you sell to him?"

Clary's inclination was to repeat that it was none of Ellen's business, but maybe if she made it perfectly clear, once and for all, the woman would leave her alone.

"For one thing, I dislike Kahn's taste in architecture. The world has enough gaudy houses without more here at the lake. I'd like to see the old places stay, including mine."

Ellen gave a derisive grunt. "Architecture, hell. That's not it, and you know it. The real reason is that you want to punish me and the others for how we treated you and Barbara. Isn't that right?"

Perhaps it was, partly. It was hard for Clary to believe she was that vindictive, but given the way she and Barbara had been degraded, she'd certainly have a right to her revenge. She'd have to examine the idea later. Right now, Ellen demanded her attention.

"Maybe we deserve it," Ellen was saying. "We were shitty to you, I know. People talked behind your back. At least I was honest. I never tried to hide how I felt about your . . . " she paused, looking for the right word. "Your relationship. If you can call that sort of thing a relationship."

Clary felt her stomach muscles knot as they always did
when she came face to face with the hatred of homophobia.

Ellen continued, "People here always liked the Hadleys, respected Marge and Dan. Growing up, Barbara seemed like a nice, normal girl. She was a tomboy, but that didn't mean anything. A lot of folks blame you for getting her started on . . . " she stopped and sniffed. "Well, you know."

"Do you want me to furnish the word, or are you simply too prissy to say it?"

Ellen's platinum hair shook in exasperation. "Stop it, Clary."

"You stop it, Ellen."

Ellen looked as if she'd been slapped in the face. Did she really expect Clary to sit back and allow herself to be insulted? Barbara had kept her from making a scene before. Now, if Ellen kept on, she'd make a big enough ruckus to alert the whole town.

Ellen picked up a menu and fanned her face. "Be reasonable, Clary. You got that property for free when Barbara died, the house and the cabins. You didn't have to lift a finger for it. The money from its sale would be pure gravy."

Clary remembered how Barbara lay dying inside that house she "got for free," remembered the long nights full of Barbara's pain and the sleepless nights full of her own pain. She remembered fetching and carrying, coaxing Barbara to eat, watching as her beautiful body grew to be little more than a skeleton. She'd begged Barbara to live, as if it were a matter of will power. And she remembered how, at the very end, Barbara didn't even have enough energy to ask for a glass of water.

She remembered bathing Barbara, touching her, kissing her, wanting to make love but afraid to bruise. She remembered the soul-killing void inside her after Barbara died.

Now, Clary drained her glass and set it carefully inside its ring on the table. "How much do I owe for the lunches?"

"That's it?" Ellen exploded. "That's frigging it? I thought you'd at least be willing to discuss it."

Clary got to her feet, waging an inner war to keep her emotions from exploding. She fished a twenty dollar bill out of her pocket and dropped it on the table in front of Ellen.

"We have discussed it."

* * * *

Outside in the parking lot, Jo mentioned that she needed gas. Cal's Garage housed the only pumps in Lassiter and that meant they'd get to see Richard. Even though he had lived at home during Jo's initial visits to the lake, he and Jo barely knew one another. He'd been so sullen and withdrawn at the time that even Clary felt as if he were a stranger.

Despite her limited contact with Richard, Jo had been

fully aware of his "growing pains." Clary had sometimes vented her frustration when the three of them had dinner together. It was cheaper than therapy, and the advice was probably more

Chapter Seven

When they arrived back at Clary's, the afternoon sun was just past its summit, and the lake glinted beneath its rays. In the winter, it often took on a grayish cast under the leaden sky, and her mood dipped in accordance. But, now, in the summer, it gave a vibrance to her life and lifted her spirits. If it hadn't been for the cast on her foot, she could have accomplished all sorts of tasks.

"Going for that swim now?" Clary asked, as they pulled up in front of the house.

Jo cut the engine and looked listlessly toward the lake. "I don't know. It's still busy on the water. I'd hate to get run over by a power boat. Maybe I'll just stay here and read. There's always tomorrow."

Lucy lay in a patch of grass, her forelegs stretched in front of her, sphinx-like. Clary distinctly remembered locking her in the house before they left and wondered if she'd escaped through the pantry window again. It had happened more than once. She'd have to remember to get a new lock for it the next time she went to the hardware store.

Jo turned the key and started the engine again. Suddenly, she shut it off and got out. "Clary, we nearly forgot the groceries."

Clary laughed. "Aren't we a pair? With all that I've got going on, I have a good reason for being forgetful. You're on vacation. What's your excuse?"

Jo said, "I'll bring them up. You go inside and rest."

As Clary mounted the steps, she noticed the garden hose strung across the veranda. She hadn't put it there, and it was certainly unlikely that John Munger had come down to water for her. Her gaze followed the hose to where it wound into the house through an open window; she heard the hiss of water pulsing through. It didn't take long to realize that someone had flooded her house.

"My God. Jo!" she called.

Jo ascended the steps at a run. "What's wrong?"

"Someone's put the garden hose in the house and turned on the water."

Jo rushed to the window, wedged her fingers in the crevice, and grabbed the hose. It snaked in her hand with the pressure of the flow. Dragging it to the edge of the porch, she fed it over the side. Standing upright again, she demanded, "Give me your keys."

Trembling, Clary fished them out of her pocket and handed them to Jo but, to her surprise, the door was open.

"They either jimmied it or came in through the window in the pantry," Clary said.

"Regardless, let's get inside. Hopefully, they didn't do any more than flood the place."

Water slid over the sill onto their feet and, inside, the polished plank floors shimmered under a layer of water. The braided rug made squishy sounds when they stepped on it. Clary stood in one place, casted foot elevated, and surveyed the room.

"I can't believe this," she said. "Who would do this?"

Jo traveled the rest of the house, looking for signs of mischief.

"Who on earth would do this?" Clary repeated as she returned.

"Your guess is better than mine. Could it be that developer getting even with you?"

"Could be. He was certainly mad enough. Marissa's a likely candidate, too. She didn't want to come here in the first place and that, added to her dislike of lesbians, might cause her to do anything. Ellen said she was out running errands. Maybe one of her tasks was to swing by here and play around with my hose while I was out."

Not that Marissa and Kahn were the only suspects. There were other people who had reason to make her life miserable: Ellen Graham or her husband, John Munger, and any number of other residents who simply had it in for her on general principles. The list seemed so daunting, she couldn't deal with it.

"What do I do now?" Clary asked Jo.

"Hike yourself outside while I telephone somebody who knows how to turn a swimming pool back into a house."

Willingly, Clary complied, resting on her crutches in the shade of a tree while Jo made some calls. She came out a few minutes later to report that she'd found a company who offered emergency flood service. They would arrive within the hour.

* * * *

Two men maneuvered a truck up beside Clary's house and unwound vacuum hoses, mumbling that they'd be done in a couple of hours. Her hardwood floors might be ruined, one of them told her, and, if enough water had seeped into the floor vents, the heating system as well.

"Can't you do something to stop it?" she pleaded.

"What do you think I am, lady, a miracle worker? The damage has already been done. All we can do now is mop up after."

Clary climbed in the car beside Jo, and they drove down to Telluride to wait. She stood anxiously watching her house from the porch, while Jo went inside to get her book. As she settled into her deck chair, Jo said, "There are magazines inside. Grab one if you like."

Clary shook her head. "Too much on my mind to concentrate. I'll just sit here on the steps and enjoy the sunshine. I can use the vitamin D."

She eased herself down, aligning her crutches beside her. Before long, the warmth of the sun took effect, and she sprawled out, leaning back against the railing, eyes closed.

Without explanation, Jo began reading aloud. Clary had no idea what had led up to the current place in the story, but she didn't care. She felt so relaxed that Jo might as well have been reading the telephone directory.

As she listened, Clary wondered why she'd never noticed the lilt in Jo's voice before. It curved with the phrasing of the sentences, lulling her into a peaceful calm. Now and then, the sound of the water removal equipment interfered with Jo's words, and Clary wished they'd turn it off. She wanted to enjoy the sweet sound of Jo's voice and savor the strange tingle traveling up and down her spine as Jo read.

Between paragraphs, Jo paused to gaze down at her, and a warmth as soothing as the sun caressed Clary's skin. She pulled the one intact leg of her pants higher and slid her shirt sleeves to the shoulder, savoring the feeling. A silence fell.

Through half-closed lids, Clary glanced up. "Don't stop
reading."

Jo put her book down and stood up. "I need to stretch for a minute."

Clary's eyes followed Jo as she paced the deck, her long legs tanned and pleasantly muscular. Her new haircut accentuated her even features, and the sunlight brought out its rich amber color and revealed gold flecks in her hazel eyes. Clary wondered why she'd never noticed their almond shape or the spray of freckles across Jo's cheeks and on her arms.

Jo stopped at the railing and looked into the trees, taking a deep breath. Sunlight silhouetted her body under her cotton T-shirt. She wore no bra, and her nipples punctuated the cloth. Clary caught her breath and sat up.

"Maybe I will get a magazine after all. Seems like we're going to be here for a while."

Jo looked down at her and smiled. "Sure you don't want me to read aloud anymore? Maybe if I sat beside you on the steps, you could hear better. That machine makes a racket."

"No, that's okay. A magazine will be fine."

Jo went inside for one, handed it to Clary, and took her place in the deck chair again. Clary turned her back and opened to an article in the middle. For the next hour or so, both women remained silent.

After a time, the whir of the machines stopped, and Clary saw the two men rewinding their hoses. Jo noticed them too, and they went up to the house.

Inside, fans and dehumidifiers had been placed to aid the drying process. One of the workmen joined them while the other finished up outside. Scratching his jaw, he looked around at the soaked floorboards.

"Can't guarantee that the wood can be saved," he said. "You won't really know for a couple of days, 'til after this place dries out. At least the heating system escaped."

"That's good. Thank you," Clary replied.

He held out a clipboard and a pen. "If you'll sign here and then give me your insurance agent's name, we'll be on our way. We'll deal with your company directly, save you the hassle of filling out a bunch of forms."

Clary scrawled her name and then went into the kitchen, opening the drawer that Barbara had

disparagingly called her "bastard filing cabinet." Buried in the pile of papers and
bills was the house insurance policy. She found the business card with her agent's name and returned to the living room, handing it to the workman.

"Just for my information, what did this little siphoning job cost?" she asked.

"Seven hundred dollars."

She tried to keep from choking. "That much?"

He shrugged. "Two hours, two men, the equipment . . ."

"It's okay. I understand. Thanks for coming so promptly."

After they left, Jo brought Clary's groceries in, putting them away while Clary wandered dejectedly around the house, surveying the damage. When she came back, Jo was standing at the door, ready to leave.

"You've had a horrible day, haven't you? I'm sorry," Jo sympathized.

"That's the way it goes sometimes."

Jo touched her arm. "I was planning to throw a meatloaf in the oven for dinner. Would you like to join me?"

Clary caught her breath. Meatloaf had been Barbara's favorite meal, meatloaf with mashed potatoes and green beans. She hadn't thought of it in ages, and she was suddenly overcome with the pain of missing Barbara. She touched her wedding ring, wondering if the day would ever come when something as small as the mention of Barbara's favorite food would not rekindle her grief.

"I'd better pass. Today wore me out. I guess I left my staying power back in that pothole. I wouldn't make very good company."

Jo lowered her eyes, clearly disappointed by the refusal. "Is that all there is to it?"

"What do you mean?"

"Today, on my porch . . . well, there was . . . "

Jo broke off, but Clary knew what she was about to say. There had been a certain energy between them, an energy that
Clary had chosen to ignore.

Never, even in her wildest dreams, had she ever thought of Jo as anything except a friend. Her friend and Barbara's friend. But, this afternoon on the porch, she'd seen Jo in a new light, seen her as a vital and attractive single woman, who, if Clary didn't guard against it, could be exciting to her in a romantic way. She couldn't let that happen. So soon after Barbara's death, she simply wasn't in a position to become involved with anyone.

She forced herself to smile. "What a way to spend the afternoon, eh? Thanks for your help and hospitality, by the way. Without it, I'd have been stuck standing outside, wringing my hands."

Jo smiled weakly in return. "I'm glad I could help."

At the door, she hesitated. "Sure about dinner? I promise I won't - - "

Clary cut her off. "I appreciate the offer. Maybe another time."

Jo nodded, pushed through the screen, and slowly walked down the hill to her cabin.

Chapter Eight

When parents are asked which of their children they love the best, they invariably say they love them equally well but for different reasons. Among other reasons, Clary loved her daughter, Karen, simply because she was female. As much as she loved Richard, there was something special about having a daughter, someone of the same gender to watch mature and grow into womanhood. Even better, they were much alike, so that, in a way, it was like watching herself grow up again.

One morning, just as Clary was settling down to read the paper, Karen phoned. Karen had just received her degree from the University of San Francisco and was soon to begin postgraduate studies. They hadn't seen one another since December at Barbara's funeral.

As soon as she heard who it was, Clary's spirits soared.

"What's up, honey? Everything okay?" Clary asked.

"Oh, sure. Now that I have my degree, a lot of the pressure is off. In fact, I'm the picture of self-indulgence, sleeping in late, gorging on ice cream, pampering myself to make up for all of those late nights I spent studying."

"You deserve it. I still feel rotten that I couldn't attend your graduation. If it hadn't been for this broken foot . . ."

"Forget it, Mom," Karen broke in. "Things happen. But I was wondering if you felt like flying down and joining me in my debauchery for a couple of days. We haven't spent time together in ages. It'd be fun, that is, if you feel up to it."

It was a wonderful idea, a way to get out of the house and reconnect with her daughter at the same time.

"I'd love to," Clary replied. "I'm not up to hiking all over town, but if you don't mind keeping the activity to a minimum, I'd be up for it."

"Great! When can you come?"

"I'll have to check the airlines."

"Perfect. Call me back as soon as you know."

As soon as she hung up, Clary hauled out the yellow pages and called several airlines. Finally, she found one that flew direct. The price was acceptable, and she gave them her credit card number and instructions to hold a seat for her on the flight out tomorrow morning. After calling Karen with the information, she dialed the garage to see if Richard could give her a lift to the airport.

He'd be glad to drive her, he said, except that the garage was jam-packed with cars to be repaired, and he didn't want to take the time off. Was there anyone else she could ask?

Jo came immediately to mind.

Clary walked down to Telluride, where her knock yielded no response. As she turned to leave, Jo emerged from the trees on the lake path. She wore a pale blue bathing suit and carried a towel, a book, and a folding chair. Her tawny hair, dark with lake water, clung to her head like a cap, and a pair of sunglasses rode atop her head.

"Hi, Clary," she said, approaching the cabin. "Come in for a glass of iced tea?"

"No thanks. I came to ask a favor."

After Clary had explained about her visit, Jo said, "Of course, I'll drive you to the airport. If you like, I could even tag along. I'd love to see Karen again. You'll have your hands full trying to manage those crutches plus baggage and taxis."

It seemed like a good idea until Clary recalled the feelings she'd experienced for Jo yesterday afternoon. Karen's small apartment would sleep only one, so she'd have to stay in a motel, and she felt unsure how to handle the arrangements. It would seem funny for her to insist on two rooms, yet for reasons she hesitated to admit, even to herself, she felt afraid to share a room with Jo.

"I appreciate the offer," she said, "but maybe you should stay here. After that incident with my garden hose, I'd feel better if you stuck around and kept an eye on things."

Jo shrugged. "Okay. Whatever you think best."

* * * *

Clary needn't have worried about traveling with the broken foot. People treated her like an invalid and anticipated her every need. She found herself tipping more generously than she could afford and hoped she'd be able to find a cheap motel after she saw Karen. She wasn't in a position to be squandering her money these days.

Karen met her at the airport in her vintage VW, and they drove directly to a small motel, where Karen had already reserved a room for her. From there, they drove across town to the Castro district where Karen lived.

Driving through San Francisco, the city where she had lived so many years ago, Clary experienced mixed emotions: the stress she'd felt trying to support herself and her two children after her husband left, and then, later on, the excitement of the first flush of love when she had met Barbara. It had all happened so long ago, yet, in some ways, it seemed like only yesterday.

At one point, they passed a restaurant that she and Barbara had frequented, and Clary let out a small sigh.

Karen took her eyes off the road for a moment and looked at her, her green eyes mirroring Clary's own. "You okay, Mom?"

Clary smiled to ease Karen's mind. "I'm fine. It's just that there are so many memories here. That restaurant we just passed, the Cellar . . . "

To her surprise, Karen burst out laughing.

"What's so funny?"

"I remember how, about every other Friday night, you and Barbara would hire a sitter and go to the Cellar. I always had this picture of you driving to someplace like the Bates Motel and descending a long, dark flight of stairs down into the bowels of the earth. What you did down there, I had no idea. I only knew that it was either illicit or, at the least, very secretive. I'd lay awake, waiting for you to come home, just to be sure you were safe."

Now, it was Clary's turn to laugh. "I had no idea. You certainly didn't think that Barbara would lead me into any kind of danger, did you?"

"Oh, no. Barbara would never do anything to put you in danger. I always knew that. She loved you so much that she had sympathy pains if you even got a headache."

It was true. For that, Clary would eternally be grateful.

* * * *

For two days, Clary and Karen talked about their lives and enjoyed one another's company. One day, they took a picnic lunch to Golden Gate Park, and the next, they pretended to be tourists and spent the day at Fisherman's Wharf. On their way home, they happened to drive past the apartment where the four of them, Clary, Barbara and the children, had lived before Barbara inherited the lake property.

Seeing it, Karen launched into a recitation of her childhood memories. They were filled with happiness and good times, and Clary added memories of her own. But long after they had passed the apartment, Clary found herself remembering a day that had not been so happy. It stuck out in her mind because it was one of the few times she had ever seen Barbara lose her temper.

Barbara had been working on a particularly troublesome chapter in her novel. Before going to bed one night, she had announced to Clary, "I'm getting up at the crack of dawn to finish that damned chapter. Come hell or high water,
it's going to get done."

When Clary got up to make breakfast, Barbara was already holed up in the closet-sized bedroom she used as her office. After driving the kids to school, Clary made fresh coffee and a plate of scrambled eggs and took them in to Barbara, who was hunched over her computer with her eyes closed and her hands folded in her lap. "Do not disturb" was written
all over her. Clary silently deposited the food on the desk and left without a word.

Throughout the morning, she returned to freshen Barbara's coffee, careful to be as quiet and unobtrusive as possible. Once, when things seemed to be moving along, she rested her hands on Barbara's shoulders and kissed the back of her neck.

"How's it going?"

Barbara grunted and shook her head. "It is going to hell in a hand basket."

Except for taking in a sandwich at lunchtime, Clary stayed away for the rest of the day.

On the way home from school, Karen and Richard were noisy and restless. Summer vacation began in a week, and the anticipation of three months of freedom had turned them into bundles of activity.

Beside her on the front seat, Karen said, "Susie at school got some lipstick. She showed us at lunch. Can I get lipstick, Mom?"

"You're too young for lipstick, Karen."

"Susie's the same age as me and her mother let her."

"No, and I'm not going to argue."

"But Mom . . . "

"I said no."

Karen pouted, giving up to Richard who read out loud to them from a book of magic tricks he'd checked out of the library. When he came to one involving sugar cubes, ashes, and a cigarette lighter, he said,

"When we get home, I'm going to ask Barbara to help me try this. Barbara's good at this kind of stuff."

Meaning that Clary wasn't.

Her tone was sharper than she'd intended. "When we get home, you are going to sit down and do your homework. Your last English essay wasn't exactly what I'd call suitable for framing."

"English doesn't count. School's almost out anyway. What do I care?"

She could have launched into a lecture that lasted all the way home, but she didn't. One person in a bad mood was enough for one household.

At the house, she said to Karen and Richard, "Barbara is working very hard today. We need to be quiet so she can concentrate, okay?"

Richard trudged off to his room, and Karen settled on the sofa to brood about her naked lips. But as soon as Clary disappeared in the kitchen to start preparations for dinner, her offspring headed for Barbara's den. She could hear them all the way across the house.

Richard: "I read about this neat magic trick. Come help me try it. I want to show my friends tomorrow."

Karen: Barbara, do you think I'm old enough for lipstick?

Richard: All we need is sugar cubes and some . . . "

Karen: Susie got some lipstick. She doesn't wear it at school, but . . . "

Clary heard a loud thwak as Barbara's fist came down on the desk. She dropped the apple she was coring and ran to the den. Barbara's voice chopped through the air like a cleaver.

"Get out of here. Both of you. I'm trying to get some work done. What I do in this room is what pays the bills. Go badger your mother."

When Clary reached the doorway, the children were coming out, Karen in tears, Richard with his jaw clenched and his eyes full of fire. Clary let them pass, then stood staring incredulously at Barbara.

A minute passed while Barbara angrily rearranged a stack of manuscript pages, and Clary wondered if the comment about who paid the bills was an indictment. It had never been an issue before. She decided not to bring it up now. Instead she said, "Dinner will be ready about six. Come join us. If you want to."

She left to pacify the children and finish up in the kitchen, being extra careful with the paring knife. The way she was feeling, she wasn't sure who she wanted to use it on the most: Barbara, the kids, or herself.

Ten minutes later, Barbara came in. Clary glanced at her, then went back to work, saying nothing. Barbara turned her away from the counter and kissed her. Clary could see that she'd been crying.

"I'm sorry," Barbara said. "I'm so sorry."

"It took me forever to calm the kids down. Karen was scared to death, and Richard is ready to run away from home."

"I know. I'll make it up to them."

Clary sat at the table, and Barbara pulled up a chair beside her, taking her hand and looking into her eyes.

"I want you to know that I didn't mean anything by that crack about me being the bread winner."

"And me being just the Mom," Clary put in, emphasis on the word "just."

"If it weren't for you, I'd be living on tuna fish and popcorn and wearing tatty clothes and staying up all night to read. Or write."

"Sometimes, you stay up all night as it is."

"Yes, but it's usually to make love to you." She kissed Clary again. "Please forgive me, sweetheart. I promise not to let that damned novel turn me into a monster ever again."

Clary smoothed her hand over Barbara's forehead and the silky hair she loved so much to touch. "You work too hard, take it too seriously," she said.

"I won't debate that, but, for now, I intend to take some of the pressure off and go for a swim. You and the kids want to come with me?"

They did, and it turned out to be one of the most enjoyable afternoons they had ever spent together.

When Clary finished her story, Karen said, "I remember missing Daddy, but Barbara made up for it, more than made up for it. Those were happy days."

"Yes, they were. I'll never forget them."

They confined their conversation to the scenery and landmarks the rest of the way home. After they pulled into the narrow garage beneath Karen's apartment, she cut the engine and looked directly at Clary.

"Your life with Barbara was wonderful, Mom, but I hope you won't close your mind to another relationship, if one comes along. You're still young. Leave room for love in your life, okay?"

In answer, Clary only smiled.

* * * *

Clary and Karen parted company at the airport with promises to phone one another and visit again soon.

Jo's Honda was waiting at the curb of the terminal when Clary came out. Clary tipped the attendant who'd carted her bag and jimmied her crutches and herself into the passenger seat, while Jo dealt with stowing the luggage. Jo said nothing until after they'd maneuvered through the airport traffic onto the highway.

"Something happened while you were gone."

Clary kept silent, hoarding her breath inside her chest. Nothing good was on the way.

"Someone set fire to your storage shed last night. It burned to the ground."

Short and sweet, like pulling a bandage off fast to minimize the pain.

Jo went on, "After that incident with your house flooding, it occurred to me that the fire might have been set deliberately. No flammables to cause it, no paint or gasoline, nothing electrical. Chief Graham came over this morning. He said he'd be contacting you soon."

Clary let loose her pent-up breath. First the flooding, now this. Whoever was plaguing her had progressed from a dirty trick to out-and-out violence.

"What time did it happen?" she asked.

"About eleven. I was in bed reading, but I had my shades up. The light from the blaze attracted my attention. When I realized what was happening, I phoned the fire department. By the time they arrived, the shed was almost gone."

"Where was Marissa?"

"In her cabin. When the firemen arrived, she wandered out in her nightgown to see the commotion. I guess the sirens woke her up."

Either that or she'd made herself invisible for a while, then waited to hear the fire engines before coming out to view her handiwork, Clary thought.

"There was so little left of the shed, it only took fifteen minutes to douse the fire," Jo said. "Your neighbor drove down. Munger stood around and watched them put out the blaze, then got back in his truck and drove away."

Clary thought of all the things she'd stored in the shed.

Her winter clothes and her tax records and her oil painting supplies. She'd been intending to move some things of Barbara's out there as well. For once, her procrastination had paid off.

When they arrived at the lake, Clary barely glanced at the charred remains of the shed as she walked to the house with Lucy nosing nervously at her legs. In addition to the odor of smoke, Clary detected a chemical smell. Gasoline or turpentine. She kept neither of these in the shed. Jo said that the fire department didn't find evidence of flammables

But even if they didn't find a container, certainly they would have smelled it.

Trotting beside her, Lucy whined.

"Not to worry, old girl," Clary assured her. "I know you were frightened, but you're okay now."

Jo helped her unpack, put the overnighter away, took out food to thaw for dinner. She'd been so quiet on the way home, Clary wondered if she blamed herself for the fire.

As she was leaving, Clary told her, "You're not responsible for this, you know. No way you could have prevented it. You did all you could."

Jo glanced away, guiltily. "I still feel as if I let you down. You've had so much grief lately. The last thing you needed was this."

"My Indian ancestors fought off the white man for decades. Should be a simple matter for me to put up with the pranks of one poor sick soul. I'll be all right. Thanks, Jo, for all you did."

After Jo left, Clary phoned Cal's Garage. Richard picked up the call.

"Just wanted to let you know I'm back," she said, "although, if I'd known what I was coming back to, I might have stayed longer."

"Everyone in town's heard about it. People seem to think it was set on purpose."

"That's what Jo thought, too."

There was a pause while Richard said something to someone in the background about a clutch before turning his attention back to her. "Who would do something like that?"

"It could have been anyone. I'm not exactly the most well-liked woman at the lake, you know." She didn't need to explain to him what she meant.

"But, burning your shed down in the middle of the night?
That really sucks."

"At least, it wasn't the house. I'll survive."

"Give me a call if there's anything I can do to help. And be careful, okay, Mom?"

"I will," she assured him.

* * * *

Later that night, Clary went outside to take her trash to the barrels at the back of the house. As she pushed aside plastic sacks to make room for the new one, she caught a whiff of the chemical smell that had lingered around the burned-down shed. Reaching down into the barrel, she found an empty gasoline can, one that had been emptied, she reasoned, in order to fuel the fire.

Clary suddenly remembered Marissa's comment about a fire if she didn't clean the oven in the cabin.

Maybe one thought had led to another, resulting in the destruction of her storage shed.

Clary tried to make sense of it. No normal person would resort to such violent behavior because they disliked lesbians. Perhaps Marissa was more troubled than Doris had let on.

Clary carried the gas can back to the house, careful to touch only the handle. If there were fingerprints on it, she would be willing to bet they belonged to Marissa.

Chapter Nine

Police Chief Harry Graham stopped by the next morning. Harry looked more like an accountant than a policeman. Clary supposed it had to do with his short stature and thick glasses, which magnified his watery blue eyes. She had often wondered what had drawn Ellen to the timid, uncertain constable. In their case, it seemed to be true that opposites attract.

They stood in the yard as Harry asked questions and wrote her answers on a lined yellow pad, intending, Clary guessed, to transfer her responses to an official form back in his office. She had a suspicion that the faster Harry could conclude his business with her, the happier he'd be. Though not as openly hostile as his wife, Harry disapproved of her every bit as much.

After the preliminaries, he asked, "Any ideas who might have set the fire? That is, if it actually was set."

"Plenty. Everyone who believes that AIDS is the remedy for homosexuality, plus the people who dislike me in particular because I won't sell my property to Gerald Kahn."

Harry winced at her outspokenness. "That doesn't narrow it down much, does it?"

"Why don't you start with Marissa Matthews?"

"The girl who's working for my wife at the Inn?"

"Yes. She's angry with her mother for making her come up here, and she's transferred the anger to me.

Wait here. I want to show you something." Clary hobbled to the porch, returning with the gas can she'd found the night before. "This was buried in my trash."

"So?"

"So, I smelled gasoline around the shed yesterday, and last night I found this empty can, suggesting that the fire was set."

"Fire department said it wasn't."

"The way I heard it, Harry, is that they didn't find any flammables in the shed. Maybe if they'd found this empty can, they'd have changed their minds. Why don't you take it and see whose fingerprints you find? I have an idea you might find Marissa's."

Harry took the gas can from her and made a note on his yellow pad. Behind the glass walls of his lenses, his eyes scanned the page. "Guess that's all for now."

Clary turned to go back in the house, then remembered.

"And, by the way, Harry, this isn't the only monkey wrench that's been thrown in my direction lately. A few days ago, someone tried to turn my house into a replica of the lake by putting the garden hose through a window. It's my guess that if you find the arsonist, you'll also have the person who did the flooding."

"Okay, Clary," he said with zero enthusiasm. Passing the charred remains of the storage shed, he called over his shoulder, "You'll have to clear away this debris. City ordinance says you can't leave it."

"Why not?" she called back. "If it doesn't bother me, what's the difference?"

"I'm only telling you the law. Do what you want. I'll be back in a couple of days to see what you decided."

She bet he would, probably armed with a citation carrying a hefty fine or an arrest warrant.

She waved him off and went inside.

Shortly past noon, Jo came to say she had errands to run in town. Did Clary want to come?

She seemed to be spending more time with Jo than she had intended after the awkward moments between them on the porch. But she couldn't resist the invitation. She could use the trip to consult with Cal about carting off the remains of the shed. He was on a long-time resident and would be sure to know of someone. She got herself ready and met Jo at her car fifteen minutes later.

On the road, she told Jo about discovering the empty gas can and about her suspicion that Marissa was the one who'd emptied it.

"Wow," Jo replied. "The kid would have to be really disturbed to set a fire just because she doesn't like queers. Are you sure that her mother didn't leave out some of the most interesting details about her background? That she's a pyromaniac, for instance?"

"Doris just said that Marissa was having growing pains. I'm sure if there was more to it, she would have told me."

"I hope so," Jo said.

Clary had Jo drop her off at the garage, and they agreed to meet in front of the post office in two hours.

As she walked onto the lot, Clary observed that the tourists had already gassed up and headed out for the day, but that the repair bays were packed with vehicles. Richard was bound to be busy during the week.

The only sign of life was Cal's dog, a two-toned beast of dubious extraction and unpredictable habits. He raised his head to track her progress across the lot, then lost interest and plunked it down on outstretched paws to nap again. Apparently, a person on crutches posed no threat.

Cal sat in his office, hunched over the handwritten pages of a ledger. When he saw Clary in the doorway, he closed the book, happy for an excuse to quit working.

Pushing out of his swivel chair, he removed his vintage baseball cap, smoothed a hand over a crosshatch of thinning hair, and indicated a chair beside his jumbled desk.

"Take a load off, Clary."

She propped her crutches against the wall and sat down.

Cal eased his bottom into the swivel chair again.

"Damned accounts," he said eyeing the ledger. "I can't make them add up half the time. The older I get, the less patience I have. I'm beginning to think it's time for me to sell this place and take up model train building. Always wanted to do that. Got no time now to do anything but run this damned business." He pushed the palm of an age-spotted hand across his jaw. "What's up, Clary?"

She explained about the fire, which he'd already heard about from Richard, and told him about Graham's ultimatum. "Harry's just enough of a weasel to put me in jail if I don't comply," she said. "Know of anyone?"

"Yeah, my nephew Hank. He's got a truck and lots of unemployed buddies to help. He's also got a brand-new baby. He could use the extra money."

"What do you think he'd charge?"

Cal sucked his teeth thoughtfully. "Around two hundred's my guess."

"But there's hardly anything left except a pile of ashes," she protested.

"Things ain't like they used to be when the kids worked for three dollars an hour, Clary."

She ought to have learned that from her experience with the water removal company.

"If you want, I'll send Hank to have a look," Cal offered. "Maybe you can talk him into a bargain rate. Smile and bat those big green eyes at him. I always had the notion you could bring men to their knees if you wanted to."

She gave him a facetious thumbs-up. Both of them knew that she'd never had the slightest interest in having men do anything for her on their knees. Except maybe fix the plumbing.

She thanked him and got up to go.

Cal creaked out of his chair, put on his cap, and snatched a set of keys off the corner of his desk. "I'm closing up to get some lunch over at the Inn. Drop you someplace?"

She checked her watch. She had over an hour before meeting up with Jo again. She remembered her depleted reading supply.

"How about the library?"

"Sure."

"On second thought, make that the drugstore. I have to meet my ride at the post office and the drugstore's a lot closer. When you're traveling on crutches," she grinned, "you learn to pay attention to those things."

"Drugstore it is."

She knew she shouldn't be spending money on paperbacks, but she had to have something to fill her time, didn't she? She was due to receive a royalty check soon, so she could afford a small splurge. Remembering the water removal company, she made a mental note to call her insurance agent and make sure her policy would cover the work.

After an hour of combing the racks, Clary settled on a mystery novel and a cookbook. Even though she rarely prepared anything more complicated than lasagne, she read cookbooks the way some people read dictionaries. She liked reading the recipes and looking at the photographs.

On the way home, Jo lowered the windows and drove slowly along the lake. At one point, she pulled off the road, and they sat for a while, enjoying the breeze and watching the water skiers. With daylight savings time in effect, it was light until almost eight o'clock, and the tourists took advantage of every last minute.

"What a treat this is for me," Jo said. "I like living in Santa Rosa, but sometimes I get a yen for the great outdoors. It's kind of like getting the urge for a milkshake when you're on a diet."

Clary nodded, smiling faintly.

Jo continued, "You're lucky to live here."

"Yes, I am."

Jo pivoted to face her. "I'm so sorry the world has turned into such a rotten place for you. You're a wonderful person, and you don't deserve any of what's happened to you."

It was true. Her life was a mess these days. As if losing Barbara weren't enough, her mind was filled constantly with money worries and, now, someone had decided to make life even more miserable by flooding her out and burning her shed down. She could use a good cry and, ideally, a comforting shoulder to do it on. But not Jo's.

Circumstances had forced them to be together more than she was comfortable with. The feelings she'd experienced that day on Jo's porch had frightened her. They were the sort of feelings she'd always reserved for Barbara. She couldn't imagine sharing them with anyone else. Especially not so soon.

No, she told herself, she'd pull through. She always managed to stay in one piece during a crisis. Whether it was really a factor or not, she attributed her resilience to her Indian blood. If she could get through Barbara's illness and death, she could get through anything.

"I'll be all right," she told Jo. "Thanks for your concern."

They remained silent the rest of the way home.

As they pulled into the yard, Clary automatically glanced in the direction of Marissa's cabin. Usually, she could detect the teenager's presence by the loud music thumping across the landscape. Today, the air contained only the sound of leaves rustling in the wind and the rat-tat of riveters from the construction on the opposite shore.

A motorcycle stood at the rear of the cabin shrouded by bushes. They noticed it at the same time.

"What's that doing there?" Jo asked.

"I don't have the slightest idea. It certainly doesn't belong to Marissa."

"Company?" Jo suggested.

"Could be. If it's male, I might have trouble on my hands."

"Maybe now would be a good time to grab your oven cleaner and go tackle that stove, wouldn't you say?"

"Good idea."

Jo parked the Honda and carried in the books while Clary checked her phone messages. The only one came from John Munger. His drawl had given way to a staccato demand.

"You call me when you get home, Clary. We got to talk."

Clary clicked off the machine, wondering about the cryptic message. Her eyes met Jo's.

"I'd better call and see what's up. Thanks for the ride."

"Anytime."

Jo left, and Clary dialed John's number. He answered immediately. From the tension in his voice, he hadn't regained his composure since leaving the message.

"That girl," he snarled, "the one from your cabins?" He stopped, his speech bottled by anger.

"Marissa? What about her?" Clary prompted.

"She came over here this afternoon with some gangster on a motorcycle. They raced up and down the shoreline, kicking up rocks and sand and yelling like banshees. Then they turned into my property. Tore the hell out of my garden. When I ran out to make them stop, the boy gave me the finger, and she called me a string of names worse than I heard in the Navy."

Clary bit her lip and said some bad words of her own under her breath. Marissa had been here just over a week and already she'd managed to get into trouble. Doris had mentioned that she was a little defiant. A stunt like this indicated more than just a little bit.

"I'm sorry," Clary said.

"Sorry is as sorry does," he snapped. "What're you going to do about those hooligans?"

If Marissa had been her child, she'd have had a ready answer. Under the circumstances, she wasn't sure.

"I'll let you know."

She hiked to Marissa's cabin, anger powering her into moving faster than she thought possible. She pounded on the door, waited, pounded again.

Marissa opened the door wearing a sleepy expression and buttoning her blouse. Cigarette smoke wafted through the screen.

"What can I do for you, Clary?" she crooned.

"Who's with you?" Clary demanded.

"What's it to you?"

"A house rule I have about underage guests not having company in their rooms."

In answer, Marissa pushed the door open and grandly gestured to someone sitting at the table with his back to them. He slouched, one leg crooked over the arm of his chair. The squared-off toe of his boot kept time to the beat of the music from the tape deck. Beside him on the table, Clary spotted a half-empty fifth of vodka and two glasses. She recognized him as the boy who'd driven Richard over the morning he came to pick up her truck.

"This is Dale," Marissa said. "We were just having a . . ." She lapsed into a giggle, obviously inebriated.

"Well, I hope you've had it," Clary said, "because it's time for Dale to go."

Marissa snorted. "You can't tell Dale what to do. You can't tell me either. You're not my mother."

"Speaking of your mother, I think we should call her with a progress report. She'll be interested in your joy ride down at the lake this afternoon. She'll probably also want to hear what you did to my neighbor's garden and your part in my shed burning to the ground."

"Hey, you don't think I had anything to do with that fire, do you?"

"I don't know, Marissa, but the police are looking into it. In the meantime, you come make the call with me. It'd be a shame for your mother to hear only one side of the story."

Marissa tossed her head, her blonde curls shaking with defiance. "Fine with me."

She marched to the table and took a drag on her cigarette, then leaned down and said something into Dale's ear. He unwound out of his chair and gave her a peck on the cheek before shuffling past Clary out the door. Marissa ground out the cigarette and followed.

Going up the hill, they heard the motorcycle roar onto the road.

"You're not getting rid of Dale that easy," Marissa said. "I'm going to see him whenever I can."

"One more thing for you to report to your mother," Clary replied.

Marissa stood in the middle of Clary's living room, fists clamped to her hips, while Clary dialed Doris's number. She answered immediately and listened silently as Clary described recent events, ending with "I can't have this sort of thing, Doris. I'm sorry, but I want you to come take Marissa home."

Doris emitted a groan. "God, Clary. This couldn't have come at a worse time. I just got a call from New York, from a hospital. My mother's had a stroke. I'm flying out in an hour. There's no way I can come get Marissa now."

Clary winced. "I'm sorry about your mother. How long do you think you'll be in New York?"

She glanced at Marissa, who'd replaced her look of superiority with an expression of rapt attention.

"I haven't the slightest idea," Doris answered. "It'll depend on Mother's condition. I promise to come for Marissa the minute I get back."

Under the circumstances, Clary felt she had no choice but to relent.

"All right. Do you want to talk to Marissa?"

"Please."

Clary held out the receiver, and Marissa crossed the room, wavering slightly. She kept her voice flat through a series of "yeahs" and "okays" and, from her lack of emotion, Clary could tell that the news of her grandmother's stroke had about as much impact on her as a drop in the Dow Jones averages.

When the conversation ended, the girl handed the receiver back, and Clary connected with Doris again.

"I'm sorry about Marissa's behavior," Doris said. "I talked to her. Maybe it'll help. I'll call you from New York as soon as I know anything."

Clary hung up, feeling used and helpless. It might be weeks before Doris returned home. In the meantime, Marissa was sure to vent her frustration at having to stay. Clary could only hope that she'd turn it inward and stay out of trouble.

She'd barely settled the receiver in its cradle when Marissa headed for the door.

"I'm sorry about your grandmother," Clary said after her.

Marissa paused, her hand resting on the screen. "She'll be okay."

"As long as we're going to be here together, you and I need to make some kind of peace . . . "

The slam of the screen cut her off in mid-sentence.

Chapter Ten

In the late afternoon, Clary stretched out on the sofa for a nap. Eerie dreams disturbed her sleep, and she awoke an hour later, groggy and irritable.

She prepared the food Jo had left to thaw, forcing down the spinach, joylessly sawing into the steak, which she'd ruined by overcooking. She put her dishes in the sink and launched into her new novel, but she was unable to concentrate. After a few pages, she'd completely lost track of the plot, and she put the book aside.

Around eight, she fell onto her bed and tried to sleep again. After dozing in fits, she awakened two hours later to the whooshing of a heavy wind. She got out of bed, stepped around the sleeping Lucy, and went into the kitchen.

Rummaging in the refrigerator, she came across an open bottle of chardonnay. She poured a glass, drank it, poured a second. The bittersweet liquid went down easily, the alcohol washing away some of the day's tension.

Idly, she wandered through the dark house, hitching along a few steps at a time on her crutches to peruse the pictures on the walls, straighten her desk, touch the figurines Barbara had been so fond of collecting. The purposeless activity reassured her. No matter what her troubles, she had her home, her gift of security from

Barbara. That is, if she could manage to keep ahead of her creditors and produce some income to support herself. The only other alternative was selling to Gerald Kahn.

Opening the front door, she wandered onto the veranda. A three-quarter moon shimmered the ferns and made stripes through the railing across the wooden deck. Warm wind quickened in the trees and bowed the wild grasses that blanketed the yard. The peace she'd felt a moment before dissipated with the energy of the wind. It disturbed the balance in her body, infused her cells with tension. She'd read that Santa Ana winds actually sent people to the psychiatrist's office, and she suddenly understood why.

She made her way to the steps, playing a game of setting her good foot inside the shadows. Step on a crack, break your mother's back. On the top stair, she settled her weight into her crutches and listened to the sounds of the lake. A night bird sang his repertoire, trilling a pattern several times, then changing to another as intricate as the one before. The lovely variety filled Clary with awe.

The cabins stood lifeless under the cloak of night, their windows silvered with moonlight, roofs as white as if snow had fallen. She felt alone in the world.

Then, from the pool, she heard the skitter of water, concentrated her listening, heard it again. Marissa? Carefully, she descended the steps and crossed the yard, paying close attention to her footing over the uneven ground. Resentment filled her. Who had appointed her Marissa's overseer? No one. Yet it seemed she had the job. She wished she were unencumbered to enjoy the clear, cool look of the landscape, to feast her eyes on the chiseled boulders, to savor the flow of clouds overhead. Instead, she had her sights on trouble.

Carefully, she made her way to the pool. At the wrought iron fence she stopped and strained her eyes to identify the swimmer. Inside, the surface of the water broke, and liquid noises splashed against the night.

"Marissa?" she called.

Getting no reply, she unlatched the gate and angled through. With the moonlight washing across it, the concrete appeared gray-green. Fallen leaves skittered in droves before the wind and piled like snow drifts against the fence. She made her way to the edge of the pool. The swimmer slithered toward her underwater, barely ruffling the surface, then came out at the shallow end.

Jo stood before her, running both hands over the slippery surface of her hair. Her slender fingers brushed water from her eyes. When she saw Clary, she smiled.

"I couldn't sleep. I don't know why. The moonlight maybe." Jo watched her for a minute, her head cocked inquisitively. "What brings you down here? I doubt you're in the habit of taking late night walks these days."

"I was getting a breath of air on the porch when I heard noise down here. I thought it might be Marissa here with Dale."

"Who?"

Clary had forgotten that Jo had left before her confrontation with Marissa and the boy that afternoon. But it was too late and she was too tired to tell Jo the story. "Never mind," she said. "I'll fill you in another time."

Jo smiled again and brushed the surface of the water with her palms. "Come in."

"With this cast? I don't think so." She turned to go.

"At least sit down and rest before you start back," Jo said. "The sound of the wind is exciting, and the sky is as clear as a bell beyond the clouds. You can see every star."

Clary looked up.

Jo pointed. "There's Orion and, to the left, the Big Dipper. See?"

Clary didn't know Orion from Jack in the Beanstalk, it would seem rude of her to go right away. She sat down to catch her breath.

Lowering herself into a deck chair, she dropped the crutches at her feet. Jo stood waist deep and looked at her for a moment, climbed the steps and leaned to grasp the legs of Clary's chair. She braced one knee against the side of the pool and pulled the chair closer to the rim, her muscles flexing under a sheen of water. Her strength was surprising. She removed Clary's sandal, her fingers lightly brushing the arch of her foot.

"Come wade. The water's warm."

Clary shook her head. "I can't, Jo. Really."

Jo mounted the steps and held out her arms, inviting. Clary saw that, instead of the blue suit, she wore a black one, a two-piece. Her skin looked pale and silky against the dark material.

Without knowing why, Clary stood, accepting Jo's support.

Jo said. "I won't let you fall."

Clary allowed Jo to help her settle at the edge of the pool. Tentatively, she submerged her good leg in the water, rested the casted one along the edge. The water felt made of oil.

She leaned back, supporting herself with her arms, and watched Jo slither away, swim back, slough water off her hair. Jo came forward and propped herself on angled arms until they were facing each other.

Jo placed her palm against Clary's cheek, slowly sliding her hand across her jaw and down her throat. Two fingers traversed Clary's collar bone, found their way to her shoulder and circled, making fire as they passed over her skin.

Clary saw Jo's eyes, questioning, and she sat stock still. In a fluid motion, Jo pushed herself out of the pool and angled in until their bodies touched. Clary trembled as the warmth of Jo's skin radiated through the cool film of water. Her lips were feathers across one cheek.

Jo's hand played gently on Clary's back, the short nails traveling her spine. The other rested at the base of her throat and pool water inched between Clary's breasts. Jo's hand followed and cupped under, one thumb reaching to caress her nipple.

Clary felt a stirring between her legs, a stirring she thought her body had forgotten. She arched her back and gave in to it for a moment. A moan escaped her lips, and she realized that it concealed a word. The word was *no*.

Pushing Jo's hand away, she scooted from the edge of the pool, started to speak, stopped to wait for her breathing to slow. Her words came haltingly.

"We can't do this, Jo," she said. "I can't do this."

Jo pulled her hand across her eyes as if to exorcise the vision behind. "Why? Why can't you?"

Clary stood slowly and gathered her crutches off the ground. "I'm flattered that you want me, but I'm not yours to have."

Jo lowered her body and scooped water onto her face, her lashes clinging together darkly.

"I didn't plan for this to happen," she said. "It just did. I believe in taking the path life leads us to follow. Apparently, you have a map of your own."

"No map," Clary replied. "I simply can't travel down dead ends to make up for a trip that ended sooner than it should have."

Jo stared at her, confusion clouding her features before understanding came. "This is about Barbara, then? You feel guilty because of Barbara. She's dead, Clary. You have to go on living. I've been attracted to you from the first moment I saw you. And the other day on my porch, I got the strong feeling that you were attracted to me, too. I can't make up for Barbara, but.."

"No, you can't," Clary cut in. "Please don't try."

Clary saw a shudder go through Jo's body, caused, she supposed, by the harsh words.

"Jo," she said gently, "you have to understand. Barbara and I were soul mates. I know it's a cliché, but I truly believe that God put the two of us on this earth to be with one another. I never loved anyone, male or female, as much as I loved her. And it was the same for Barbara. You're right. She's gone and I have to go on living, but it will be a very long time before I feel ready for a new relationship. I'm sorry."

She pushed away from the edge of the pool and gathered up her crutches, laboriously swinging her body into them. Without looking back, she set out for her house. From the silence behind her, she knew that Jo was watching, not moving a muscle.

It wasn't until she'd gone through the gate that Jo called, "Do you want help back to the house?"

"I can make it alone. I need the practice."

Listening to the furious upheaval of water behind her, Clary made her way cautiously toward the house.

The night bird continued to trill his endless song.

Chapter Eleven

When Clary awoke, the wind had died to a gentle breeze and the thermometer on the porch read seventy, a good five degrees lower than on the last few mornings by this time.

She fed Lucy, then put together a ham-and-cheese sandwich and ate it sitting on a bench outside. She could see Marissa's cabin, its door closed. No work today, not on a Sunday. She'd either holed up inside or walked to town. Clary meandered down to Tahoe to see.

As she drew near, a voice behind her called, "Looking for me?" It came from the swimming pool.

She pivoted on her crutches to see Marissa lying on a lounge chair in a bathing suit that might as well have been left off for all the coverage it provided.

As she made her way to the pool and stood shielding her eyes against the glare off the water, Marissa raised up on an elbow and removed her sunglasses.

"How about I just set out flags for you?" she said, an edge to her voice. "You know, a green one if I'm at work, yellow if I'm inside alone, and red, definitely red, if I have company. That way you won't have to bother looking in the windows."

"I wasn't looking in your windows, Marissa."

"I'll bet it crossed your mind though." She replaced the sunglasses and lay back on the lounge.

Clary said, "It looks like we're stuck with one another for the time being. It'd make things easier if we could get along. I don't want to snoop in your business, but you force me to when you pull stunts like yesterday's."

"I guess the trick is to keep you from finding out then," Marissa replied without moving.

Clary bit her tongue. If she allowed herself to engage, things would only get worse.

"I'm not exactly having the best time of my life right now. I can do without added aggravation. Your mother sent you here to help you. It's clear you're not happy, but why not make the best of it?"

"There's no best of it to make. Being watched by a dyke gives me the creeps. We've got plenty of fags in San Francisco, but not right next door."

Clary's throat constricted. She wondered where Marissa had acquired her bigotry. Not from Doris. Maybe it simply came with being heterosexual and fifteen. Or maybe it was a ploy to goad Clary into leaving her alone to do as she liked.

There seemed no point in continuing the conversation. Clary turned to leave.

As she shut the gate, her gaze fell on Telluride. No sign of the Honda, no sign of any life. Either Jo had driven to town or she'd gone home. It'd be a bitter way for their friendship to end, but perhaps it was to be expected after last night.

Clary settled on the porch and tried again to read the mystery she'd abandoned. She had managed to get to chapter six when a truck rumbled down the drive and cranked to a halt beside the house. Two men got out, and while one of them started tossing shovels out of the back, the other sauntered up the steps to talk to her. A minute later, her old Ford rolled in with Richard behind the wheel. He parked her truck near the house and squatted down beneath a tree to wait while she conducted her business.

"I'm Hank, Cal's nephew," the man said. "You got something to haul away?"

Clary pointed to the shed. "What would you charge me?"

Hank walked down for a closer look, conferred with his buddy, then came back to the house. "Two fifty," he told her.

"That's practically the down payment on a house," Clary protested.

He shrugged, gave her a look meant to convey his steadfast resolve, and remained silent. No dickering here.

"I'll think about it," Clary said.

"I couldn't come back until next weekend. I work full time. You ain't going to get it done for less."

Clary considered that. She made a sweeping gesture out over the yard. "See those weeds?"

"Yeah."

"Knock those down to ground level too, and it's a deal."

"No problem."

Hank hitched up his pants and went down the hill to start work.

Richard, who'd been watching them from his spot under the tree, walked up to the porch, hanging back at the edge. "When I heard the guys were coming, I decided to return your truck and hitch back with them."

"Thank you. I still can't drive yet, but hopefully it won't be long."

"Thanks for letting me use it." He hesitated for a second. "Could I talk to you, Mom?"

"Sure. Come in the house. It's getting hot out here."

He followed her to the sofa and took a seat on the ottoman facing her. Elbows on his thighs, he clasped his hands, prayer-like, beneath his chin. Whatever he had on his mind held importance for him. He took a deep breath and looked squarely into her eyes.

"Cal's decided to sell the garage and retire. I'd like to buy it. The bank won't give me a loan, so Cal's going to carry me, carry the paper I guess is how they say it. Only thing is, he wants thirty thousand as a down."

Clary opened her mouth to speak, but he plunged ahead, talking fast.

"I never would have asked you before, not with all the trouble I caused you, but I've really been trying, Mom. I haven't missed a day of work since I started at the garage. Cal says I'm a good mechanic. I can fix almost anything. People around here'd come to me, people from Metcalf too. And then there's the tourists. I've got it all figured out. I could make payments to Cal and you both, no sweat."

The pleading in his voice made her catch her breath. She was reminded of a time when he was nine and convinced that his life would end if he didn't get an expensive drum set he'd seen. At the time, she could barely afford to put food on the table. He'd come up with a list of chores to earn the money. She knew it would take him a lifetime and prayed that she could come through at the last minute. But she hadn't been able to. It had broken his heart and hers as well.

She knew that she was about to break his heart again.

"I'd like to see you get the garage, honestly I would. But … "

He dropped his head. "But you're not going to give me the money, are you?"

Clary could see that he was fighting back tears, and she had the urge to take him in her arms and rock him the way she had when he was a child. He wasn't a child now, though, and she wanted to help him preserve his dignity.

"I'd give you the money if I had it, Richard. I don't."

He looked puzzled. "I don't get it. You've got the rent from the cabins, and the royalties from Barbara's books, and the child support money."

"For heaven's sake, Richard, use your head. I stopped getting child support the day you turned eighteen."

"Oh, yeah," he said, as if that had never occurred to him, which it probably hadn't.

"The cabins are a seasonal business, and after Jo and Marissa go home I don't know who I'm going to rent them to. And, as wonderful as her books are, Barbara's royalties really don't amount to a whole lot. I didn't want to worry you with it, but I'm having a difficult time getting along these days. Once my foot is healed, I plan to try selling my paintings. And, they said they'd hold my job at the hardware store. But right now . . . " She broke off in frustration.

Richard's face reflected a sobriety she had never seen before, and he came to her and took her hand in his. "Gosh, Mom, I didn't realize things were so tough for you. I just assumed . . . Well, I assumed wrong, I guess."

She rubbed the back of his hand against her face, feeling the downy hairs on her cheek. "I didn't mean to bother you with my troubles," she apologized. "You caught me at a bad time. I'm having to fork out over two hundred dollars to Cal's nephew for clearing away the shed. I'm not the one you should be asking for money today."

"I'm sorry, Mom. I'll just have to come up with another way to get it. Maybe this isn't my time to go into business, anyway. I'm still young. There'll be other chances."

Clary hoisted herself up on her crutches and followed him to the door.

Before going out, he said slowly, "I know this is none of my business, but people in town say that Kahn has offered you a real good price for this property. I guess you don't want to sell?"

"No, I don't. This is my home, Richard, the only home I've ever really known. Barbara and I shared it for thirteen years, and you and Karen both grew up here. I can't imagine living anywhere else. You can understand that, can't you?"

"Sure, I can. Even if you wanted to move away, I wouldn't blame you for holding out against someone like Kahn."

"He's not exactly my favorite people," Clary replied.

"Him and that goon, Carl Smail. They act like they own the town."

After Richard left, Clary thought about what he had said. If things got any worse for her and she couldn't hold out, Kahn and his cohort might very well own the town. She had lost more than a few battles in her life, but losing this one would affect her more than she cared to think about.

Chapter Twelve

Richard spent the next few hours helping Hank and his friend clear away the debris from the shed and whack down weeds. They finished around five o'clock, and while Richard and the other man opened cans of beer under a shade tree, Hank came for his money.

Clary wrote out a check, praying for it not to bounce. Doris Matthews had paid her only a portion of Marissa's rent. Now that she'd gone to New York, the rest might not be forthcoming for some time. She should have mentioned it when they spoke on the phone, but somehow the subject of money had seemed out of sync with the rest of the conversation.

Jo owed her money too. Clary dreaded having to ask for it, but she dreaded even more writing rubber checks. She decided to swallow her pride and go see Jo. That is, if she hadn't gone home.

It took Jo several minutes to answer the door. Clary noticed that, instead of her customary shorts and sandals, she wore a pair of khaki pants and hiking boots. A spray of freckles fanned across her cheeks where the sun had coaxed them out, and fresh suntan colored her throat and arms. Her fingers flew to smooth her disheveled hair when she saw Clary, telling in their nervous energy.

"Sorry to bother you," Clary said. "Something's come up and I wondered if you could pay your rent."

"Of course," Jo said quickly. "I should have taken care of it the first day."

She turned into the house and came back with a check, handing it through the half-open door. "Does that bring us up to date?"

Clary noted the amount. "It looks right. Thank you."

"Well." Jo stepped back, signaling the end of the conversation.

Reluctant to leave on the note of strain, Clary said quickly, "I'm doing laundry tomorrow. Do you have anything you'd like me to throw in?"

"Not that I can think of." Jo started to close the door, hesitated. "On second thought, I have a towel you can wash. I used it as a knapsack for some sandwiches today, and it smells of tuna fish."

She got the towel and gave it to Clary, who held it to her nose, pretending repulsion. She smiled at the exaggeration, but the smile was unreturned.

"What were you doing with tuna sandwiches in a towel?" Clary asked.

"Hiking in the mountains. I had some thinking to do. Being outdoors helps."

"It's nice up there this time of year."

"Yes."

It was obvious that small talk would not dissolve the barrier between them.

"Jo, about last night - - "

"Forget it, Clary. I got the picture. You're a one-woman woman, and Barbara was the woman. The last thing I want is to push myself on you. It's not my style."

Before Clary could reply, Jo had shut the door.

* * * *

Someone from the hospital in Metcalf phoned the next morning, reminding Clary that she was scheduled to come in for X-rays today. It'd been over a month, and the foot needed to be checked. They'd be seeing her at eleven o'clock.

"I'll try," Clary told her. "I can't drive, so it's a matter of finding a chauffeur."

She hung up, wondering who to ask. She didn't want to bother Richard, and Jo was definitely out. Clary had tried to show Jo that she still wanted to be friends, but from her response Clary doubted they could ever patch up their differences. Norma Latham was her only hope.

Even though Norma functioned as the town crier, she had a good heart and a generous spirit. She'd been the one to scoop Clary off the road when she'd had her accident and had taken her to the emergency room. And it wasn't the first time that Norma had helped her out.

When she and Barbara had first moved in, several neighbors had driven by to welcome them. But as soon as people figured out their relationship, Clary and Barbara couldn't ignore the chilly reception they received. Even the people who had known Barbara and her parents for years had snubbed them.

Norma, on the other hand, went out of her way to greet them on the street, to be cordial when they came into the store. When Barbara died, Norma had wept openly at the funeral and visited Clary the next day, bearing a casserole and a basket of fresh fruit. If there was anyone at Lake Lassiter Clary felt she could trust and call on for help, it was Norma.

Now, Clary put aside her laundry and phoned the grocery store. Yes, Norma said, she supposed she could make the trip. Her son, God bless his indolent soul, owed her a favor. He could very well run the place for a few hours. She'd just gas up the car and be right over.

An hour later, she floated her big Roadmaster up to Clary's door, and they set off for the hospital.

On the way, Norma kept her radio tuned to an oldies station, the music serving as background for her running comments about people and events in Lassiter. Eventually, as Clary knew she would, she got around to Clary's own affairs.

"Richard's certainly upset about losing his chance at the garage," she said. "I guess his age is the reason the bank is hesitant to make him a loan. Used to be that a person's word was as good as his bond, especially in a small town like this. Times have changed, I suppose."

"Yes, I suppose they have," Clary said.

Norma drove in silence for a while. "Of course you'd be perfectly willing to help him out if you could, I know that, dear. I can't imagine any mother refusing her own son. Your expenses must be straining you."

"You don't know the half of it," Clary replied. "I can barely keep the cabins rented, and I owe the hospital a bundle because of this broken foot. Then there's . . . well, never mind the rest. Let's just say that I'm not exactly flush these days."

Norma clicked her tongue a half dozen times, shaking her head as she clucked.

She seemed to have an endless fund of information, which she parceled out to Clary as she drove. In addition to
Richard's request for money, she knew about the fire, right down to the exact length of time it had taken the firemen to arrive, and also about the flooding of the house. It failed to surprise Clary in the least when she brought up Jo Taylor.

"She's been coming to the lake for quite a few summers now, hasn't she?" Norma said.

"Eleven, to be exact."

"I recall seeing her at Barbara's funeral. She seemed very distraught. I remember how she rushed out of the church, tears running down her face 'til you'd have thought her heart was breaking."

"Jo and Barbara were very close. She took Barbara's death very hard."

Norma drove in silence for a few minutes before saying,

"I always thought she was a pretty woman. I was struck by it again when the two of you came in the store the other day."

Clary said nothing, resenting what she interpreted as Norma's attempt to discover Jo's sexual orientation. If she found out, it would be the subject of gossip all over Lassiter.

Norma was not about to be put off by Clary's silence.

"She's a single person, like you, isn't she?"

Clary hadn't considered herself to be a single person since the day she moved in with Barbara.

"Yes, Jo's single," Clary replied shortly.

Norma's eyebrows peaked above her bifocals. "Ummm."

Nearing the hospital, they discussed how long Clary's examination might take. Since there was no telling, Norma suggested they allot two hours. That'd give her plenty of time for a good chat with her sister, who lived not far away. Unfortunately, it would also condemn Clary to a lengthy wait if the exam took less time, but she couldn't very well complain. She was, after all, on the receiving end of Norma's generosity.

Norma eased the Buick to a stop in the hospital's loading zone and waited while Clary fumbled with her purse and the crutches, finally depositing herself on the curb. They agreed to meet in front of the hospital, and Norma drove off.

Clary made her way to the orthopedic department and, within an hour, had been X-rayed and had discussed the results with a doctor. The fractured metatarsals were mending satisfactorily, she said, but not enough for a walking cast. They'd give it two more weeks and take more X-rays. Clary hoped that Norma would be willing to make the trip again.

She decided that an hour was a long time to read the year-old magazines that littered the waiting room. If she were better able to ambulate, she'd go snooping in the art stores or the garden supply, but Metcalf's main shopping center was blocks from the hospital. The thought of trying to get there on crutches seemed daunting. It looked as though she was stuck with the magazines after all.

In the middle of an article about how to give a successful baby shower, Clary remembered the bar down the block where she and Barbara had sometimes stopped in. It offered cheap drinks and good food. What better place to kill time? That is, if it was still there.

She left the hospital and made her way down the street, delighted to find the place still in existence. Although not as prevalent as in the old days, police harassment of gay bars still persisted. After receiving citations for trumped-up violations, many of them moved or went out of business. The ones that managed to survive for more than a couple of years in the same location were legendary.

The nondescript building sat on the corner, it's only identification a small sign above the door reading "Calypso Sally's." Inside, the sounds of easy listening music wafted from a jukebox in one corner, while ceiling fans designed to look like steamboat paddles stirred cool air through the big room. Plants cascaded from baskets everywhere. Flanked by a wall of mirrors, a dance floor took up one whole end.

The place was crowded for a weekday. Couples filled the booths, and singles spilled over at the bar. A gaggle of gay men occupied one end of the room, but the majority of the customers were lesbians. Dyke heaven. Several waitresses skated about, bantering with the customers while they took orders and served up drinks and food.

A big butch, who Clary seemed to recall went by the name of Skeeter, poured drinks at the bar and good-naturedly insulted everyone within earshot. She could get away with it. She owned the place and generously dispensed advice to the regulars about everything from income tax problems to rocky love affairs. Clary knew because on one occasion she and Barbara had been privy to her comments while nursing beers nearby.

Clary found an empty booth and settled in. When the waitress came, she ordered a corned beef sandwich and a screwdriver. Normally, she didn't drink during the day, but with the way life had been going for her lately, she owed herself a little relaxation. Norma might be able to detect corned beef on her breath, but not vodka.

Waiting for her food, Clary found herself twisting her wedding ring and wishing Barbara were here. Almost everything she did seemed joyless without her. A redhead in a sundress came out of the restroom and paused beside her booth, making eye contact. Clary smiled and shook her head. The redhead moved away.

The music stopped between songs, and the room quieted suddenly, as rooms tend to do when something changes. In the silence, a woman's laughter sprinkled the air. Casually, Clary looked around for the source, which turned out to be a table on the outskirts of the dance floor. Her heart knocked wildly in her chest as she recognized Jo.

She wore light-colored linen trousers and a simple white blouse. She'd slicked her hair back into a style that imitated the DAs of forty years ago. It emphasized her cheekbones and sliced years off her age. The girl across the table looked to be about twenty-five although, without the heavy makeup, she might have appeared closer to twenty.

The girl placed a cigarette between her lips and leaned forward for Jo to light it. One hand shielded the flame

and touched Jo's. She blew out the match and smiled. Before it extinguished, Clary saw that Jo wore no makeup, her freckles even more pronounced than the day before. Even without lipstick, her mouth looked full, her eyes deep under naturally
dark brows.

The girl seemed to be telling a joke, gesturing and smiling as she talked. Jo laughed and crossed her legs, resting an ankle on the top of one knee and her chin on the heel of her hand. Clary had never seen her use that body language before, and it disturbed her. It was almost as if she were playing butch to the girl's femme.

Suddenly, for some reason, or maybe for no reason at all, Jo turned and looked at Clary. Her expression remained static, as if she'd expected to see her there. She rested her gaze, eyes as neutral as if she were looking at a photograph. Then, without so much as a nod, she turned back to her companion.

Clary felt her muscles tense, and she suddenly felt like the last kid on the playground to be picked for a team. She studied the things on the table: the salt shaker with a dent in its metal cap, petals from the jar of daisies dotting the tablecloth, a matchbook with a phone number scrawled in red ink across its cover.

The waitress came with her order, and she looked at the sandwich and knew she couldn't swallow one bite. She placed
a ten dollar bill under the salt shaker, gathered up her crutches, and started back to the hospital.

Clumping down the street, she remembered Jo's comment about taking the path life leads us on. Jo had merely found a new path, as she had every right to.

It shouldn't affect me, Clary thought. It shouldn't affect me at all.

Chapter Thirteen

Clary tried to analyze her reaction to seeing Jo with the woman in the bar. Part of it, she supposed, was her disappointment that Jo would stoop to a common pick-up. The women she'd brought to the lake were people she had met hiking or at her book club. Clary prickled at the idea of Jo seeking easy companionship. But disappointment was only a part of it. Much as she'd like to deny it, she'd felt jealous. But why? She and Jo were just friends, if they were even that after what had happened at the swimming pool the other night. Jo could pick up as many women as she liked, fill her little black book with as many names and her bed with as many bodies as she liked. It made no difference to Clary. Barbara had been the love of Clary's life -- and always would be.

With only a few more minutes to wait for Norma, Clary sat on a bench outside the hospital and observed the change in the weather. The sky had turned to slate, and angry clouds boiled across the horizon. Norma pulled up just as rain began to dot her hood.

"Can you believe this?" she asked, as they inched into traffic. "Rain like this in the summer? We used to be able to predict but not anymore. It's that greenhouse effect they talk about."

The greenhouse effect had little to do with weather patterns, but Clary didn't feel it was up to her to assume the role of an authority.

Comfortably situated in the slow lane, Norma took her eyes off the road and glanced at Clary's cast. "What'd the doctor say about your foot, dear?"

"It's healing as it should. She wants to check it in a couple of weeks."

By the time they reached Lake Lassiter, the rain was coming down faster than the windshield wipers could keep up. Norma constantly adjusted her glasses and repeated, "Can you believe this?"

Thunder rumbled across the sky, and lightning sliced through the black clouds. At one point, Clary suggested they pull off the road and wait for the downpour to subside.

"Oh my, no," Norma said. "If we stop, we'll be a sitting duck for the next bolt of lightning."

Were you in more danger sitting still than on the move? Clary wondered. She made a mental note to check the encyclopedia when she got home. Maybe she was wrong about the greenhouse effect, too.

At the turnoff to her house, she said, "Would you mind stopping at the mailbox? I haven't checked it for days."

Norma came to a stop, and Clary rolled down her window and tried to reach the inside of the box by stretching as far as her arm could reach. As luck would have it, she came six inches short of connecting.

Norma clicked her tongue. "I'd try to get closer, but I'd hit it. For sure I would."

"That's okay."

Clary opened her door, set her casted foot in the mud, and reached in for her mail. After grabbing the contents, she got back in the car. Even in those few seconds, she was drenched. Norma rolled down the drive, looking askance at the water dripping off Clary onto her leather seats. To her credit, not a critical word passed her lips.

At the house, Clary tucked the mail into the waistband of her pants to free her hands and struggled up the steps. Norma adjusted her glasses and inched the Buick across the yard. Clary's "thank you" was lost to the sound of the storm.

Thank goodness she hadn't locked the door. Fumbling with keys in this downpour seemed unfathomable. Inside, Lucy bounded toward her, tail happily fanning the air. Clary eased an arm off one crutch to pat her silky head.

"Thunder scare you, old girl?"

Lucy fanned her tail faster and followed Clary to the bedroom, where Clary peeled off her clothes, dropping them in a soggy heap on the floor. Cocooned in a robe, she dried her hair, grabbed her mail, and carried it to the kitchen. Over a cup of coffee, she riffled through the stack.

In addition to the inevitable bills, she'd received a flyer exhorting her to upgrade her heating system before winter and a plain white envelope with her name typed across the front. It bore no address or postage. It had obviously been hand delivered.

She extracted a square of folded newsprint. Smoothing it open, she saw *Metcalf Monitor* at the top, along with today's date. Scanning the copy, she realized that it was the obituary section. At the end of the column, she read:

> WEBB, CLARISE, passed away June 24 at the age of 42. She is survived by her daughter, Karen Ingersoll, her son, Richard Ingersoll, and by many loving friends. "Clary," as she was known, was a resident of Lake Lassiter for thirteen years. Memorial service to be held at the Pineview Mortuary in Metcalf on June 27.

Clary read the notice a second time, then a third. "My God," she muttered.

Heart pounding, she located the telephone directory, looked up the number for the *Monitor*, and punched it in. The voice on the other end held the same charisma as the recorded time message.

"*Metcalf Monitor*. Help you?"

"I want to speak to someone about an obituary," Clary said.

"That'd be Frank Hill or Dodge Cramer. Which one do you want?"

"I don't care. Dodge Cramer."

Anyone named Dodge was bound to know what was going on.

"Hold on. I'll see if he's around."

Clary waited and in a few seconds Dodge boomed, "Help you?" in a voice as deep as the Grand Canyon.

"My name is Clary Webb. My obituary's in the morning edition of your paper. I'd like to know who placed it."

There followed a cavernous silence. Finally, "Excuse me?"

"Didn't you hear me?"

"Yes, but I don't think you meant what you said."

"I meant exactly what I said. Your newspaper carried my obituary this morning. I want to know who's responsible."

"Just a moment, please." Rustling sounds came through as Dodge handed the receiver to someone else.

"Ledger, city editor. May I help you?"

From the voice, Clary was unable to determine if the editor was male or female. She took a chance on the status quo.

"Mr. Ledger, my name is Clary Webb, and I want to know who put my obituary in your morning edition."

She was beginning to sound like a broken record.

"Can you hold for a second?"

She stifled a retort about the dead being unable to hold for anything while muffled voices in the background attested to a joint inquiry. Presently, Ledger came back on.

"That particular obit, your obit," his voice wobbled. "It was dropped off yesterday. Typed, no signature." Wanda down at the front desk said that was kind of strange. Most of the obits are phoned in."

"Then Wanda saw who brought it in?"

"That was the other strange thing. She said it was a teenage kid, blonde girl she hadn't seen around before."

Clary reined in her anger. "Does your newspaper normally accept obituaries from anonymous contributors?"

Ledger packed his voice with as much authority as possible. "It's never happened before, so we had no reason to question the authenticity."

"I am the reason to question it," Clary exploded. "I am authentically not dead. I am alive, and I am madder than hell."

"We'll print a retraction in tomorrow's edition," he offered.

"You do that. Deceased by the power of the pen, revived the next day by same. Wonderful."

"I'm sorry, Ms. Webb."

"Not as sorry as I am, Mr. Ledger."

She slammed the receiver into its cradle and got up to lace her coffee with a generous helping of the scotch she reserved for colds. First, her house was flooded, then the storage shed was burned to the ground, and now this, which in her mind, was the most insidious of all the incidents.

Whoever was trying to run her out of town had gone too far this time. Proof or no proof, she had to do something to stop the harassment. She decided to call on the law. Again.

Chapter Fourteen

Clary waited 'til nine o'clock the next morning to put in a call to Police Chief Harry Graham, thus giving him plenty of time to drink his coffee, polish his boots, and settle at his desk with the newspaper. He wasn't going to be exactly thrilled with another complaint from her, and she wanted to be sure he was as relaxed as possible before making it.

"If you're not too busy today, could you stop by?" Clary asked him.

Harry released an anguished sigh. "If it's about your storage shed, there's no news."

"It's not about that. Something else has come up."

"If it's really important," he said grudgingly.

"What time can you come by?"

"Let me see."

The pause that followed was no doubt calculated to make her think he was checking his appointment book. To justify his existence, Harry even penciled in the time he spent waiting to ambush speeders.

"Can't tell you exactly," he said presently. "Sometime before noon."

"I'll be here."

At exactly eleven fifty, Harry drove his motorcycle up to the house, dismounted, and pushed the kickstand into the mud. Clary watched out the window as he ambled toward the house, squaring his shoulders and setting his jaw, as if he were going into battle. Instead of his usual khaki uniform, he wore a streamlined hunter green number with jodhpurs and knee-high boots. A revolver rested on his hip. Clary jutted a thumb in its direction as she let him in.

"Expecting action at high noon?" she asked, tongue in cheek.

Suspicion registered in his myopic eyes. "What do you mean?"

"You know, the old movie where Gary Cooper confronts the bad guy in the middle of Main Street?"

Harry stuck out his chin defensively, like a kid who'd been caught without his homework. "I've probably seen it. Don't remember."

With his best John Wayne swagger, Harry followed her into the kitchen and perched on the edge of a chair. His eyes darted around the room like nervous guppies.

Adam's apple bobbing, he cleared his throat. "Glad to see you decided to clean up that rubble. I'd have hated to cite you."

The hell you would, Clary thought.

She left the thought unsaid. "Coffee? Soda?" she offered.

"No. Thanks. Having lunch soon." The Adam's apple took another trip up and down his throat. "What's on your mind?"

"My sanity."

"Beg pardon?"

"Someone is out to scare the hell out of me. Maybe worse."

Harry crossed his legs, resting one polished boot atop the other knee. "If you're talking about your shed, you're blowing things all out of proportion. We're not even sure the fire was set."

"Did you check out that gas can I gave you, look for fingerprints?"

He avoided her eyes. "I'm working on it, Clary. Identifying fingerprints can take a long time."

"There's more than just the shed," she said.

Harry's eyebrows peaked with curiosity, and he fished a small spiral notepad from his shirt pocket and clicked his ballpoint pen.

"What?" he asked.

She reminded him about the flooding and stated her belief that the person who did that and the one who burned down her storage shed were probably the same.

He kept his face blank as he made notes. From where she sat, Clary couldn't make out the words, only that they were written in the pinched script characteristic of people who doubted their own judgment.

"So, you think the person who flooded your house also torched your shed?"

She observed the space between his eyebrows and his hairline and decided that the myth about high foreheads and superior intelligence was just that - - a myth.

"Does it seem logical that I'd have three incidents within such a short period of time all perpetrated by different people?"

"What's the third thing?"

"If you read the *Monitor* yesterday, you might have seen my obituary. It was put there by an anonymous contributor."

"You mean your own death notice was in the newspaper?"

"Yes, that's what I mean, Harry."

He wrote that in the notebook.

"I interpret it as a death threat," she went on. "Aren't death threats against the law?"

Harry passed his hand in front of his face as if to bat away a fly. "Oh, come on Clary. It's not illegal to place an obit in the paper, not even as a practical joke. 'Course in light of your recent troubles, it probably wasn't just a joke. I wouldn't go so far as to call it a threat, though. Still, I'd question the person if I knew who it was."

"The newspaper said the person who delivered it was a blonde teenage girl. For some strange reason, Marissa Matthews came to mind. Of course, she could have been put up to it by someone else. But maybe this will help."

Clary reached in her pocket and pulled out the envelope with the clipping inside and tossed it down in front of him.

"There's my personal copy. It came like that in the mail, hand delivered. You go to detective school, Harry?" she asked, not bothering to hide her sarcasm.

"Of course." The words were laden with indignation.

"They teach you about fingerprints?"

His head bobbed emphatically. "I get the message. I'll check." He took the envelope gingerly by one corner and stood, hiking up his pants. "Even if I get a clear reading, that doesn't mean I'll know who they belong to. The only prints on file belong to people with criminal records. I don't know a soul around here with a record."

"How about Gerald Kahn?"

Harry rubbed his chin and nodded. "Yeah, maybe. Nobody knows much about him, but he does have a motive for harassing you. It's no secret that you've refused to sell to him and that he's pretty pissed off."

"You might check up on Carl Smail, too," she offered.

"Naturally," he said, as if he'd already thought of it.

Harry closed his notebook, and she followed him to the door. She watched as he crossed the veranda and descended the steps to his motorcycle.

"You'll let me know what you find out?" Clary called.

"Of course."

On her way inside, she couldn't help but wonder if Harry might not find it in his best interests to ignore any evidence he might glean about Kahn. He had been careful not to reveal his vested interest, but Ellen had made it abundantly clear that they'd sell to Kahn in a minute if the opportunity arose. If Kahn were found guilty of harassment, he'd have to abandon his efforts to obtain Clary's property, leaving the Grahams out in the cold. Clary decided that if she caught Harry neglecting his duty she'd make a very big fuss about it. But, of course, she wouldn't catch him. Harry wasn't the brightest person in the world, but he was bright enough to cover his tracks.

* * * *

The next day, Clary had another try at sketching beside the road. The landscape was still scrubbed fresh from the rain, and the air smelled sweet. She lingered on her log seat long after she'd finished the drawing, enjoying the sunshine, savoring the opportunity to be outdoors and forget her troubles.

As she packed to go home, a white Mustang convertible rounded the bend and slowed at her turn-off. The man behind the wheel could have passed for a young Tony Curtis; his passenger was Karen. The car stopped and Karen bolted out, almost knocking Clary off her feet with an exuberant hug.

"Oh, Mom, I'm so glad to see you." She tightened the hug. "You don't know."

Clary pulled back, overwhelmed by the greeting. "I'm glad to see you, too. How long can you stay?"

"A couple of days. Jim's on his way to see his parents over in Glenview, and I took the opportunity to hitch."

Clary eyed the convertible and the hunk behind the wheel. "New boyfriend?"

"Don't I wish. He's engaged to my best friend." She pulled Clary into another embrace. "Why don't you go with Jim in the car? I'll walk down and meet you."

"What, and miss out on the only exercise I get? It'll take some time, but I'll catch up."

Karen got back in the Mustang, and Clary trailed them down the hill. At the house, she watched as the boyfriend-who-wasn't unloaded Karen's suitcase. She approached him and stuck out her hand.

"Clary Webb. Thanks for chauffeuring Karen. I don't get to see enough of her anymore."

He squeezed her hand politely. "My mother says the same about me." He looked at Karen. "See you in a few days? I'll call."

Karen nodded, and Jim rolled up the drive.

Walking to the house, Karen noticed the charred foundation of the storage shed. "What happened?"

Not wanting to spoil the happiness of their meeting, Clary decided that now wasn't the time to launch into an explanation. "I'll tell you about it later."

Inside, Karen took her bag to her old bedroom and changed into a pair of shorts and a tank top. She emerged with Lucy on her heels, engaging in a one-way conversation en route to the kitchen, where Clary was making lemonade. Clary observed that, at twenty-one, she still had the angular figure of a twelve-year-old. She was lucky; she hadn't inherited Clary's tendency to put on weight as she aged.

They took their lemonade to the table near the window overlooking the lake.

How's your foot?" Karen asked.

"Doing fine. If it's not all shriveled up when the cast comes off, I can keep wearing my sandals."

Karen barely grinned and, from the strained look on her face, Clary sensed that she had something on her mind. It surfaced with her next sentence.

"Mom, I got a newspaper clipping in the mail yesterday."

She scrutinized Clary's face. "Do you know what I'm talking about?"

"Damn it!" Clary exploded. "The son of a bitch is not only terrorizing me, he's terrorizing my kids too."

Karen leaned forward and patted her mother's arm to calm her. "I couldn't reach Richard, so I just came. I was so upset. I was afraid if I drove my own car, I'd run into a ditch." She took a deep breath. "What's going on, Mom?"

There seemed no point in glossing things over. Clary filled Karen in on the flooding and the fire. She tried to sound as matter-of-fact as possible so as not to alarm Karen any more than she already was, but as she talked, the growing concern on her daughter's face told her that her efforts had failed.

"You've got to do something to stop it," Karen said when she finished. "You talk as if they were only harmless pranks, but it seems to me that someone wishes you real harm. Do you have any idea who?"

Clary named Gerald Kahn, supplying her reason for suspecting him. As an afterthought, she mentioned Ellen Graham too, pointing out that their long-time animosity had only been exacerbated when Clary got in the way of her desire to sell her property.

"I wouldn't put anything past holier-than-thou Ellen," she said.

"Have you called the police?" Karen asked.

"Harry Graham's working on it, but I don't know how concerned he really is."

Karen said, "Until this thing is resolved, why don't you come home with me, stay in a motel until this nut gives up? I start classes soon, but we could spend some time together, share meals at least."

Her last visit to Karen's had put enough of a dent in her bank account. She could ill afford to do it again.

"Oh, honey, I can't leave now. I have guests in both cabins, and the one just out of braces demands all my attention."

She filled Karen in on Marissa, going into some detail about the incident with Munger, the wayward boyfriend, and the family crisis that kept Doris from coming to take Marissa home. Even though Karen and Jo had become friends when Karen was a teenager and Jo had visited, Clary avoided any mention of her. At some point, the two of them were bound to run into one another. Clary hoped she'd be absent when it happened.

True to form, the afternoon turned unbearably hot. Karen insisted on cleaning and doing the pile of laundry atop the washing machine, and, although Clary protested, they both understood that she was merely being polite. While Karen worked, Clary settled down to read and soon drifted into sleep. She awoke to sounds coming from the kitchen and went to find Karen bent over a steaming pot, wielding a wooden spoon.

"Bubble, bubble, toil and trouble," she intoned.

Karen started at the unexpected voice and lowered the lid.

"You surprised me, Mom. How was the nap?"

"Marvelous. Bet you can't say the same about the cleaning."

"It wasn't that bad." She gestured to the pot. "Pasta for salad. I'll chill it and throw in your leftovers. I brought along some wine and a loaf of good sourdough bread. We can eat outside."

"All that for a mother who was pronounced dead just three days ago?"

Karen smiled. "One thing that kept me sane was knowing that, if something had really happened to you, Richard would have called."

"That's true. By the way, Richard told me that Cal is going to retire and put the garage up for sale. Richard wants to buy it. The hitch is the thirty thousand dollar down payment. Richard asked me for it, but I'm strapped. Frankly, sometimes I'm not sure where the next grocery money is coming from."

Karen frowned. "Gosh Mom, I didn't realize things were so tight for you. Maybe I should postpone my classes and get a job to help you out until you can get back on your feet." She smiled. "I mean that both literally and figuratively."

Clary knew from personal experience that if Karen didn't get her Master's degree now, she probably never would. She had no idea how, but somehow she'd have to come up with the money.

"Let's not talk about it now," she said. "Maybe some time when we're not about to eat."

When the pasta salad was finished, Karen set places for them at the picnic table under a stand of oaks in the yard. A cool breeze lifted the edges of their placemats and ruffled the surface of the lake. They ate and talked until the sun became a semicircle of crimson at the lake's edge.

When they'd emptied their bottle of wine, Karen asked, "Shall I go get another one?"

"Why not?"

As Karen disappeared into the house, Clary swiveled on the bench for a better view of the lake and spotted Jo coming up the hill, her gait slow and casual. Clary knew that she'd probably seen them and decided that Jo had been hoping for Karen to spot her and come down, the better to avoid an awkward meeting.

To Clary's chagrin, Karen emerged just then and, seeing Jo, let out a whoop. "Jo! Come on up." She turned to Clary. "Mom, why didn't you tell me Jo was here?"

Clary kept silent and stared down at her empty plate as Jo rushed up to envelop Karen in a hug.

"How long have you been here?" Karen asked.

"Long enough to become as relaxed as a cat. I would have come along to San Francisco, but your mother thought it best for me to stay here."

Clary avoided Jo's eyes and studied the bubbles in her wine, the big ones rising to the top to burst, the small ones clinging merrily to the sides of the glass.

Eyes still downcast, she said, "We agreed that Jo should keep on the look-out for my tormentor. Otherwise, I would have brought her."

"Sit down, Jo, and tell me what you've been doing," Karen said. She picked up the bottle of wine she'd brought. "Of course, you'll have some wine with us. I'll go inside and get another glass."

She ran up the steps, leaving Clary and Jo alone.

After a protracted silence, Jo said, "I know what you think about me in that bar. It wasn't what you imagine. I was bored and wanted someone to talk to, that's all."

Clary forced lightness into her voice. "You don't have to explain yourself. I was just a little surprised that you didn't come over and speak to me. But, then, it looked as though you were having a pretty good time without me. The girl you were with was easy to look at, and I got the idea that she was intrigued with you, too."

Jo shook her head and sighed. "You're making way too much out of it, Clary. As I said, I just wanted a change of scenery and someone to shoot the breeze with. We got to chatting at the bar and ended up having lunch together. As soon as we were finished, she went her way and I went mine. I know it looked like a pick-up, but I don't go in for that sort of thing."

Clary knew she should end the conversation and leave well enough alone, but something egged her on. "You couldn't prove that by me."

"What do you mean?"

"It always looked to me like you did go in for that sort of thing. If I wanted to, I could come up with the names of a dozen different women you've brought up here to the lake."

"Mostly, they were people I knew, not pick-ups. You probably won't believe it, but I wasn't even sleeping with most of them. They were simply friends."

"What? Maybe two out of twelve?"

Clearly disturbed, Jo got up and turned her back to Clary, facing into the wind as she pushed her fingers through her copper hair. "What difference does it make?"

"I didn't hear what you said," Clary said.

Jo turned to face her. "I said, what difference does it make whether I slept with the women I brought up here or not? What difference does it make to you what kind of sex life I have? You're obviously not interested in me, so why should I explain my actions to you?"

Clary felt as though Jo had slapped her face. She wanted to tell Jo that she *was* interested in her, that she found her attractive, even beautiful, that she cared for and admired her, that she liked being close to her. And, more than anything, she wanted to tell Jo that she was frightened to death that a relationship would develop to make her feel that she was betraying Barbara.

She wanted to tell Jo, but she couldn't. She was saved from trying when Karen came out with the extra glass, happy and smiling, and totally unaware of what had taken place in her absence.

They sat for another hour while Jo and Karen babbled about Jo's job at the pharmacy and about Karen's graduate studies. Clary stayed out of the conversation.

At one point, Karen asked, "Are you okay, Mom? You're so quiet tonight. You usually have a comment about everything. Not that you're opinionated or anything." She laughed and looked for Jo to add to the good-natured teasing. When she didn't, Karen carried on with the conversation, seemingly unaware of the tension between the two women.

Chapter Fifteen

Closing up the house for the night, Karen drifted through the living room, pulling blinds and turning off lights. Before dousing the last lamp, she turned to face Clary, her brows drawn in a frown.

"What's going on with you and Jo?" she asked quietly.

Clary's heart sank. Karen was fond of Jo and, if Clary shared their differences, she would put Karen in the middle.

"I don't know what you're talking about," she said evasively.

Karen crossed the room and sank down on the ottoman facing her. "The chill between the two of you tonight was colder than a snowstorm in Alaska. Did you have an argument or what?"

Should she make up a story or tell Karen the truth? She'd never gone out of her way to talk to Karen about the details of her love life, but she hadn't concealed them either. They'd always shared whatever was necessary to maintain their close relationship. This was obviously a situation that called for sharing.

"I'm afraid," Clary said, "that Jo has indicated she'd like more from me than just friendship."

She waited while Karen processed what she'd said.

"You mean she'd like you to be lovers?"

Clary nodded.

Karen beamed. "Mom, that's wonderful. Aren't you happy?" When Clary failed to answer, Karen continued,

"Jo is a wonderful person, interesting, caring, intelligent. You're attracted to her, aren't you?"

"That isn't the point," Clary said, more sharply than she'd intended. "I am simply not ready to have a love affair. I'm perfectly happy keeping my own company, and I have enough on my mind at the moment without a new romance."

Karen shook her head. "I'm afraid I don't get it, Mom. You need a friend more than ever right now. Along comes Jo, someone you've known for years, someone you admire and like, someone who desires you. What's the real reason behind your reluctance?"

Clary rested her palm against Karen's cheek and looked into her eyes.

"Barbara is the reason."

Karen leaned into Clary's hand and closed her eyes. "I thought that might be it. You feel as if you'd be betraying her."

"Something like that."

Karen released a pent-up breath, choosing her words carefully. "I have no right to question your feelings about Barbara. And I'm not going to. But would you think about something?"

"Of course."

"Consider how much you're going to miss in your life if you dismiss Jo. Think about the joy and the love you'll be passing up. We only go around once, as they say, and it would be nice to know you're getting the most from your ride. Will you give it some thought?"

"All right."

"Promise?"

Clary nodded.

Karen kissed her and stood up. "I'm going to bed."

In her bedroom, Clary lay awake for a long time, thinking about what Karen had said.

* * * *

The house was quiet when Clary awoke the next morning. Karen wasn't in her room or anywhere else in the house, and Clary's truck was still parked in the yard. Unless Karen had walked to town, Clary's next best guess was that she'd gone to visit Jo.

She got dressed and took a bagel and a cup of coffee out to the porch to wait. Karen showed up a half hour later, wearing a bathing suit and carrying a towel draped over her shoulder. She mounted the steps and settled beside her mother in the porch swing.

"Jo and I took an early swim," she explained, breathless from the uphill climb. "Kind of a spur-of-the-moment thing. You don't mind, do you?"

"Of course not. I'd feel bad if our differences affected you. Spend as much time together as you want to."

Karen gave her a peck on the cheek. "I'm glad you feel that way. Knowing how things are between you, I won't invite her up to the house, but I'd like to spend some time with her before I have to leave."

"I understand."

After Karen dressed and downed a bowl of cereal, they drove into town. Karen bought a lipstick at the drugstore, and they stopped by Cal's garage so that she could say hello to Richard. Richard had the day off, Cal told them, and a list as long as your arm of things to do. Little chance of catching him at home, either. Karen would just have to see him some other day.

Arriving home, the truck bumping over the ruts in the yard left by the storm, Clary sensed that something was wrong. She couldn't pinpoint what, but she'd experienced the same prickling sensation on the back of her neck before and had learned that it usually meant trouble. Unfortunately, her ESP was right on target.

They found Jo kneeling beside Lucy at the base of the steps. She stood up quickly when they got out of the truck, and Clary saw that she was trembling. On the ground, Lucy writhed, her limbs twitching, deep in the throes of muscle spasms.

"I found her like this a few minutes ago," Jo said. "It looks like poison."

"We still have a vet in town, don't we?" Karen asked Clary.

She nodded her head, speechless.

Karen bent down, scooped Lucy into her arms, and ran for the truck.

"Mom, come and show me the way. Jo, keep an eye out, okay? "

Jo helped Clary get in the truck while Karen eased Lucy into her arms and then climbed in behind the wheel. It was a good thing that Harry wasn't watching for speeders that day, because Karen drove at least twice as fast as the limit allowed.

They reached the offices of James Hitchcock, DVM, within ten minutes and parked in the red zone out front. The place was empty except for the receptionist, a twitchy little woman who looked like she'd pass out at the sight of a fever blister. She escorted them directly to an examining room and summoned the doctor. He came running from the back and started his examination in his shirt sleeves, directing Clary and Karen to wait outside, where they sat in the reception area and pretended to read magazines for a half hour.

When the doctor emerged, he wore a white coat and a relaxed demeanor.

"Looks like a case of snail bait poisoning," he said. "She's old -- what's the dog's name?"

"Lucy," Clary supplied.

"Lucy's old, but she'll survive. Good thing you got her here quickly. I pumped her stomach and administered fluids. I'll keep her overnight just to make sure."

He stroked his chin, and Clary noticed that he was missing the pinkie finger on his right hand. Apparently, it wasn't a problem.

"May I ask you something?" He stuck the three-fingered hand in his pocket and went on without waiting for an answer. "Why'd you put out snail bait with a dog around? Most critters have the sense to shun it. Not yours, apparently. Didn't it occur to you?"

"I never use snail bait," Clary said staunchly.

The doctor looked dubious. "Then how'd the dog come by it?"

"I don't know, but I'm going to do everything I can to find out," Clary replied.

She knew full well that she had as much chance of that as she had of finding out who had flooded her house, burned down her shed, and placed her obituary but, when it came to an attack on an innocent creature, her indignation spurred her to a heightened resolve.

They were allowed to go back and tell Lucy goodbye, after which Clary wrote out a check and told Dr. Hitchcock she'd return for the dog in the morning. She and Karen returned to the lake, still shaken, but in a decidedly happier state of mind than when they'd left.

At the house, Jo rushed to the truck before they were halfway out.

"How's Lucy?"

"Thank God, she'll be okay," Clary replied, angling out on her crutches and pushing the door shut with an elbow. "You were right about the poison. Snail bait. They pumped her stomach, and she has to stay overnight."

"You didn't see anyone around after we left, did you?" Karen asked.

"I walked through the woods and along the lake, but I didn't see anything suspicious. I didn't think the culprit would hang around for long."

"You'd better tell the police about this," Karen said.

"Why bother?" Clary replied. "This is exactly like the other incidents. Without catching the nut red-handed, there's no way to prove a thing. I'll just have to keep my eyes and ears open and see if I can pinpoint the culprit myself.

"Although," she added, "it doesn't take a genius to narrow the field. Whoever hurt Lucy is definitely one of the people who's angry with me for refusing to sell this property."

Karen nodded.

"But, enough of that," Clary said. I need to go sit someplace and baby this leg. For some reason, it feels ten pounds heavier than when I started out this morning. Any more excitement and I'll have to get a crane to lug it around."

* * * *

Jo returned to her cabin, Clary lay down for a nap, and Karen settled at the kitchen table with a textbook. Just as Clary was drifting off to sleep, she heard raucous music coming from Marissa's cabin. Angered by the intrusion, she climbed out of bed and headed for the cabin.

As Clary passed by, Karen looked up from her reading. "Nap over so soon?"

"It didn't even get started. How can you study with that racket outside?"

"What racket?"

So much for the young and their ability to tune out.

She found Marissa in a lounge on her porch, reading a paperback. An imposing black boombox sat beside her, the volume turned up high enough to vibrate the deck.

"Would you mind turning that down?" Clary shouted.

Lazily, Marissa reached down and punched the radio into silence with a scarlet fingernail.

"How can you concentrate with that?" Clary asked from the foot of the steps.

Marissa lowered her book, resting it on her bare midriff, and turned sleepy eyes on Clary.

"I can't concentrate wihout it," she said. "It sort of like breaks up the monotony."

Clary switched gears. "Did you go to work today?"

"What do you think? Every day except Sunday. Why?"

"Somebody came around today and gave a dose of snail bait to Lucy. I thought you might have seen them."

Marissa's expression softened. "Oh, no. Someone poisoned your dog? She didn't die, did she?"

Marissa's concern seemed genuine, and Clary was surprised. "No. We took her to the vet, and it looks like she's going to be okay. Did you see anything suspicious around the place?"

Marissa puckered her mouth and closed one eye, thinking. "Not suspicious, exactly, just strange. I came home for lunch 'cause the greasy food at the Inn is like getting to me, you know? And, well, that grouchy old man from up the way showed up while I was eating."

"John Munger?"

"The old guy with the garden and the nasty temper. He was getting in his truck as I came out to go back to work."

"Did he say what he wanted?"

"No, and I didn't ask. He's not like my idea of someone to rap with, you know?"

"Did you see Lucy around?"

"No."

Marissa hitched her shoulders to her ears to signal that she'd said all she was going to, lifted her book, and began to read. Clary walked back to her house, wondering why John had come. For a fleeting minute, she entertained the thought that he might be her tormentor. Like Ellen Graham, he'd never made any bones over the fact that he disapproved of her but, unlike Ellen, he hadn't gone out of his way to embarrass her or to cause trouble. When he'd come over that day to talk about Kahn's offer, he hadn't seemed highly motivated to sell. She wondered, though, why he'd come by today.

Going up the steps, Clary smiled to herself, picturing the scene when Marissa and John encountered one another in the yard. Al Gore meets Cinnamon Spice! It was the first amusing thought she'd had in days.

Chapter Sixteen

After another swim, Karen returned from the lake to make dinner. Clary stayed out of her way, using the time to put in a call to the veterinarian. Lucy was fine, he told her, resting comfortably. She should be fit as a fiddle by tomorrow and could go home anytime after nine.

It was still light when Karen set the picnic table, and they settled under the trees to eat. Ravenous after the day's stressful episode with Lucy, they polished off their food in no time. An easy breeze played through the leaves of the oaks as they watched the sun lower behind the horizon.

While clearing the table, Karen said, "Would you mind if I went down to Jo's after I finish the dishes? She invited me to come for ice cream sundaes." Her voice became artificially casual. "You're invited too, by the way. She asked me to tell you."

It occurred to Clary that Jo was using Karen as a go-between, to repair their damaged relationship. Jo had seemed almost ready to make up the night Karen arrived, but today, she'd been aloof, even in the midst of Lucy's crisis.

"You go ahead," Clary replied. "There's a movie on TV I'd like to watch."

Karen cast her eyes downward in disappointment. "Jo really would like you to come, Mom. We talked about the two of you this morning. Jo said she wanted me to understand the tension between you. I told her you'd already explained it. She isn't upset anymore. I wish you'd accept her invitation."

"I don't think so."

Karen shrugged. "Have it your way."

After Karen left, Clary changed into her favorite oversized T-shirt and settled down in front of the TV. It took only a few minutes for her to realize that the movie was a waste of time, and she decided to go to bed. She switched off lights, leaving one on for Karen, and remembered to leave the front door unlocked. On her way to her bedroom, she heard the front door open and went back to say goodnight. By the time she saw Jo, it was too late to withdraw.

"The mountain to Mohammed," Karen said, holding out a sundae.

Irritated that Karen had brought Jo, knowing how Clary felt, Clary said crisply, "It's a little late for dessert. I was just going to bed. I'll see you in the morning."

"Sit down, Mother."

The sharpness of the command startled her. Before she could respond, Karen went on, "Jo and I would like to talk to you. Can you spare thirty seconds?"

Karen's uncharacteristic sarcasm was not lost on Clary. Dutifully, she walked to the table and sat down, leaning her crutches against the edge. Karen and Jo pulled out chairs, and Karen pushed the dish of ice cream toward her, like a parent trying to placate a child. Clary scooped a dollop of whipped cream off the top and waited.

"We think you're in danger, Mom. Including this incident with Lucy today, you've had four horrible things happen to you lately. It's clear that someone wants to scare you away. Jo filled me in on that developer, and it sounds as if he has enough at stake to go to any lengths to get this property, including bodily harm to the person in charge of the access road, which happens to be you."

"I don't know if it crossed your mind or not," Jo added, "but the attempt on Lucy's life today may have been a dress rehearsal for what's in store for you."

Clary put her spoon down, no longer interested in the ice cream. Obviously, Jo and Karen had talked at length about this. She had an idea what they were leading up to, and she didn't want to hear it.

"First of all," she said calmly, "I don't know if Kahn's threatening me, or if it's someone else. He isn't the only one who'll gain if I sell. I have several greedy neighbors, like John Munger and Ellen Graham."

"Who'd sooner cut her wrists than step on Lucy's tail," Karen scoffed. "Everyone knows she loves animals. Can you picture Ellen setting fire to your shed? She'd worry about breaking a nail lighting the match."

"How about Marissa?" Clary asked. "You haven't had the pleasure of meeting her, but Jo can tell you what a delightful creature she is. Homophobic from the get-go and madder than hell at having to be here. I wouldn't put anything past her."

"You don't know the half of it," Jo said. "I have a friend who's high up in the San Francisco school system. I gave him a call and found out that Marissa was expelled from school for being drunk in class last year. Also that she committed assault on her mother because Doris grounded her for having failing grades. Since you're one of Doris' best friends, it's an easy stretch to see how the kid might take out her violent tendancies on you."

Karen stood up, scuffing the chair legs on the floor. As she spoke, her voice climbed half an octave and the veins in her neck stood out. "The point is, Mother, it doesn't matter who's playing these dirty tricks on you. Whoever it is means business. You seem determined to ignore the danger you're in. You've always been so damned obstinate ... "

Attempting to ward off an all-out argument, Jo cut her off. "Karen's worried about your welfare, just as I am, Clary. Despite our differences, I care about you. I think . . . " She glanced at Karen. "We both think you should sell this property and move before something really bad happens to you."

Clary leaned back in her chair. "I know that you're both looking out for my welfare, but I am not going to sell. Barbara wouldn't have wanted me to any more than I do."

"Despite the fact that your life may be in danger?" Karen demanded. "Regardless of the fact that you can hardly pay your bills? I don't know what this Kahn guy has offered you, but my guess is that it's enough for you to dig your way out of a lot of debt. Why don't you just forget your pride for once and do the sensible thing?"

Karen was right, at least about being able to get out of debt. Things were getting worse all the time, and Clary hadn't a clue how to fix them. Still, there must be a way. She just hadn't come up with it yet.

"I think we've talked enough about this," Clary said. "I'm going to bed."

With that, she got up and went into the bedroom, leaving Karen and Jo to talk about her foolish obstinacy all they wanted to.

In the morning, Clary and Karen carefully avoided talking about the episode while they got ready to drive into town for Lucy. By nine thirty, the house was a sauna, and as they walked to the truck, the sunbaked ground sent up waves of heat like flames. As they neared the vehicle, Marissa sauntered out of Tahoe in a tank top and a pair of skimpy shorts.

Karen unlocked the truck, turning her head to look at the girl before opening the door. "Is that the charming young lady you're so fond of?"

"In the flesh. She works at the Inn until four each afternoon, but I don't believe the experience is doing much to improve her attitude. She's still just as snotty and obnoxious as the day she arrived. Well, almost," she amended. "When I told her about Lucy, she seemed genuinely concerned. A person who likes dogs can't be all bad. Maybe there's hope."

The way Karen had parked the truck made it impossible for Marissa not to pass close by. She raised her eyes as she came alongside, paused, but said nothing.

"Can we give you a lift?" Karen offered.

"No thanks."

She fixed her gaze on Karen, obviously curious. Grudgingly, Clary introduced them. "Marissa, this is my daughter, Karen. She's visiting from San Francisco."

Marissa hiked an eyebrow. "Your daughter?"

Clary wondered about the question and decided it was connected to some belief Marissa probably had that lesbians didn't have children. She looked at Marissa squarely. "I have a son, too. Your mother was his teacher when you lived here."

"I guess I was too young to remember." She shuffled her feet, her face alive with unasked questions. "Well, I'd better go to work."

"Sure you don't want a ride?" Karen asked. "It's pretty hot for walking."

"I don't mind."

Inside the truck, Clary asked Karen, "Did you notice how surprised she was to discover I have kids? I'll bet she also thinks that black people all tap dance and eat fried chicken three times a day."

"And that all Hispanics belong to the Catholic Church," Karen said.

"And that all lesbians either hate men or wish they were men and that the Irish drink too much and that Asians are geniuses when it comes to math and science."

They burst into laughter. They were still laughing as they passed Marissa going up the drive.

They retrieved Lucy from the veterinarian's office and put her between them for the ride home. The old dog lay her head in Karen's lap, flopped her tail against Clary's arms, and then sat up, looking happily out the window.

"Look, Mom, she's smiling."

"And well she should be. Someone up in doggy heaven spared her life."

"Just as someone up in people heaven has spared yours so far," Karen rejoined.

Clary ignored the warning.

Karen suggested they stop at the garage again so that she could say hello to Richard. She hadn't seen him since Christmas and might not get the chance again until next Christmas.

As they drove to the garage, Clary thought about last December. Barbara had been admitted to the hospital by then, and Clary had spent the major part of every day and night at her bedside. In her absence, Karen and Richard had been left alone in the house. It hadn't been a very festive time for them.

"Last Christmas was one of the hardest times I ever had to endure," Clary mused now. "Even though I couldn't spend much time with you, it helped just to know you were there."

"It was hard for me too," Karen said. "I thought my heart would break every time you went out the door to the hospital. It did break the night you called home to say Barbara was gone. I hope she knew how much I loved her. Having her as my second mother made my life twice as rich. I have you to thank for bringing her into my world."

"No," Clary said quietly. "You have Barbara to thank for bringing both of us into her world."

They pulled into the garage, and Clary stayed in the truck while Karen went to find Richard. They connected in one of the repair bays and hugged, engaging in a flurry of conversation. Clary studied the weeds growing on the side of the lot and, when she looked again, Cal had taken over Richard's job, and he and Karen were walking down the sidewalk, talking. It looked as though she might have a long wait.

A few minutes later, John Munger pulled up to the pumps and jammed a gas nozzle into his old pickup. He noticed Clary and lifted his chin in a silent greeting. When his tank was full, he pulled out, parked at the side of the building, and came over to Clary's truck. Through the open window, he looked past her to Lucy.

"Dog does your driving these days?" he asked dryly.

"My daughter's driving. We stopped so she could visit with Richard for a few minutes. We just picked Lucy up from the vet's. Someone tried to do her in with a dose of snail bait yesterday."

She scrutinized John's face for signs of guilt.

"You don't say." Munger stuck a tentative hand through the window to pat Lucy, who lowered her head and nuzzled Clary's arm.

"Ain't it time to put an end to these malicious pranks?" he asked. "From what I hear in town, you've had your share. When it comes to the family pet, I'd be concerned."

"I am concerned."

Munger rubbed his stubbled cheek. "Maybe you ought to sell your property to Gerald Kahn and move yourself out of harm's way."

"It's been suggested more than once. Even Karen thinks I should give in."

"And?"

"So far, I'm not ready to go that route."

He chewed on his bottom lip. "For myself, I've definitely decided to move, that is, if I can get rid of my place. Kahn's made me a good offer, not as much as yours, I don't guess, but enough. I wrote my son and he wants me to come back to Iowa. He's got a kind of cottage on his land for me to live in, and I reckon I can rustle up some of my old cronies for company. Easy enough change to make except for one thing."

"I suppose that would be me."

"You know it. You and the access road. Some of us ain't too happy about you blocking Kahn. Your stubbornness is getting in our way. I'm sure you know that. We had a little get-together over at the Inn the other night, just me and the Grahams. If one of them's responsible for your grief, they didn't let on. Anyway, we agreed that if money was the thing, we'd be willing to throw in five thousand each to help change your mind. Would you be interested?"

"Not in the least."

He stepped back and kicked her front tire with the toe of his boot. "Goddamn it. What's it going to take with you? Does someone have to . . . "

He broke off and rubbed his fist over his face and eyes in frustration. "You're riling up an awful lot of people, Clary."

"Frankly, I couldn't care less," she said.

He turned on his heel and stalked to his truck. When he was a few feet away, Clary called, "Marissa said you came down yesterday. Was it to talk about this?"

He seemed taken aback. "Kid don't miss nothing, does she? Yeah, I wanted to talk about this."

He got in his truck, screeching out of the lot just as Karen and Richard appeared from their turn around the block. As Karen got in behind the wheel, Richard leaned in the window, kissed Clary on the cheek, and reached past her to pat Lucy on the head.

"Hi, old girl. How you doing? Feeling better today?" He said to Clary, "Karen told me about the snail bait. Think it has anything to do with the other nasty things that have been happening to you?"

"I wish it didn't, but I'm afraid so."

He tilted his head. "Maybe you should take Kahn's offer and get out of here while you still can. You're the only Mom I have. I don't want to see you in an early grave."

"Oh, for heaven's sake. Nothing's going to happen to me. One thing I'm not is a coward, and I'm not letting some bully drive me out of my house."

He shook his head and turned away to resume work.

As Karen started the engine, she said, "Was that John Munger I saw talking to you?"

Clary nodded.

"About selling your property?"

"What else? We've never been exactly the best of neighbors. It wouldn't have surprised me a bit to find a few anti-lesbian epithets spray painted on the side of the house when Barbara was alive. Now, it seems his rancor has been increased over my refusal to sell my property."

Karen pulled out into traffic. "Have you . . . ?"

Clary was weary of talking about it. "Forget it, Karen. I really think we've discussed this enough."

Karen set her mouth in a tight line and drove back to the house in silence.

Chapter Seventeen

When they arrived home, they found a phone message from Karen's ride, Jim, saying that he and his parents had run out of things to talk about and that he planned to return to San Francisco the next morning. Karen called him to set a time and, when she hung up, her mouth was drawn down and her eyes were rimmed with tears.

"What's the matter, honey?" Clary asked.

"Oh, Mom," Karen wailed, rushing into her arms. "This hasn't been a good visit for us, has it? First, that awful obituary and then Lucy being poisoned. On top of it, you and Jo not getting along. It's terrible."

Clary pulled her close and kissed her forehead the way she used to when Karen was upset as a child. "Oh, honey, don't worry about it. Shit happens, as they say."

Karen's laugh merged with a sob and was smothered in Clary's shoulder.

"You'll come back for Christmas, won't you?"

"Sure, Mom. I wouldn't miss it."

"We'll make up for it then, okay?"

Karen pulled out of her arms and wiped her tears away. Her face brightened a little. "Let's make our last night special. Think you could hobble down to the lake for a barbecue? We have steaks and corn in the husk.

We could take the old hibachi. Remember how we used to do that, you and Barbara and me? It'd be fun."

"It would be fun," Clary agreed. "You carry the gear, and I'll carry the crutches. Seems a fair division of labor to me."

Karen laughed. "Yeah, right."

An hour later, with Lucy loping ahead, they walked down to the lake and settled on a section of shoreline where the gravel had been pummeled into sand and the water slapped against the beach. Clary sat in a folding chair, watching Karen play chef and calling encouragement to Lucy as she tried to catch small fish at the water's edge. The lake still brimmed with activity and, as they waited for the coals to die down, they entertained themselves by watching the swimmers and boaters down at the public docks.

By the time the corn husks had blackened and the steaks had broiled to a perfect medium rare, the summer people had left, and they had the place to themselves. They ate heartily, slipping chunks of meat to Lucy. Satisfied, they sprawled on the blanket and witnessed the miracle of the sun slipping behind the trees, melting into the horizon.

As they packed to go, Jo wandered into view, her eyes on the ground as she picked her way over the rocks and the chunks of debris that had washed ashore. So great was her concentration, she didn't see them.

"I might not get to see Jo again before I leave," Karen said. "I know you'd probably rather not have her around, but would you mind? For me?"

It would be selfish for Clary to refuse.

"It's fine, Karen."

Karen called out, "Jo, there's an ear of corn left. Come take it off our hands."

Jo looked up, smiled, and then walked up the sand, stopping a few feet from the edge of their blanket. Her short hair was ruffled from the wind and her sunglasses rode atop the waves of curls like a pair of dark surfers. She wore walking shorts over her bathing suit and a man's white shirt, unbuttoned, tails flapping out behind her. In contrast, her skin showed deeply tanned.

"I've had my dinner, thanks," she replied. "How's Lucy?"

"See for yourself." Karen pointed to where Lucy was bounding through the trees toward them. She slid to a halt beside Jo, furiously slapping the air with her tail and lifting her broad head for pats.

"She looks great," Jo said. "You'd never know she'd been sick."

"Especially if you'd seen her wolfing down meat," Karen laughed. "Our handouts probably added up to a couple of whole steaks."

Karen and Jo sprawled on the blanket to talk, while Clary sat off to one side by herself and pretended to study the water. When it became too dark to see well, Jo helped Karen gather the cooking gear and carry it up to the house. They deposited the hibachi in the yard to cool and carted the rest into the kitchen, dropping everything haphazardly on the counter. Karen dumped the paper plates in the trash and ran water to wash the utensils.

"Stay and talk a while," she urged. "I have to leave tomorrow morning. This might be the last chance we have."

Jo picked a dish towel off the rack and began drying the glasses. "Good timing. I'm leaving in a day or two also."

"So soon?" Karen asked. "You usually stay longer than this."

Clary noticed that Karen glanced in her direction as she spoke, no doubt guessing that Jo's departure had something to do with their strained relationship and wondering how Clary would take it. Clary tried to keep the emotion she felt from showing on her face.

"I have a few chores to do before I go back to work," Jo said, "and I thought I'd better not procrastinate."

Clary concentrated on putting things back in the refrigerator. When she was finished, she disappeared into the living room to read, trying not to think about Jo's leaving. She had to go home sometime. Now was as good a time as any. It would end a chapter in their lives, though it wasn't a particularly happy ending. But then, real life chapters didn't always end like the ones in novels. She'd have to accept it.

She plugged through her book with the chatter from the kitchen as background. Once, Karen came in to ask if she wanted dessert. No thanks, no room, Clary refused. Karen went back to the kitchen. Jo made no appearance at all. Clary read another chapter and by then it was almost ten. Marking her place, she put the book aside and crawled into bed. The murmur of conversation came to her through the walls as she closed her eyes. She obviously wasn't missed.

* * * *

She awoke the next morning to the sound of talking and laughter coming from the living room. In her sleepy haze, she thought it might be Karen and Jo still engaged in last night's conversation, but a man's voice dispelled the idea, and she decided that the voice belonged to Jim. Afraid that Karen had decided to let her sleep and might leave without saying goodbye, she quickly threw on a robe and hobbled on her crutches to join them.

Jo, Karen, and Jim sat in the living room drinking coffee. After good mornings all around, Clary got a cup of coffee for herself and took a place on the sofa, feeling like the only girl at the prom without a date. She took little part in the conversation, recognizing it as the useless stuff people engage in to fill time before parting, and when Jim announced that they definitely had to be going, she felt relieved.

Jim carried Karen's suitcase to the convertible, leaving her to say her goodbyes. She kissed Clary, hugged Jo, and rushed out the door, trailing advice about taking care of themselves and keeping in touch. From the bay window, they returned her wave and watched the car go up the driveway and turn out of sight down the road.

"Well," Jo said, packing the monosyllable with finality. She took her empty coffee cup to the kitchen and walked to the door, back straight, steps definite.

"You don't have to go home early because of me," Clary said. "There's lots of space between here and your cabin. No reason at all for us to run into one another."

"I know, but I really do have things to do before I start the daily grind again. The lake will be here for the next time."

Clary lowered her head, avoiding Jo's eyes. "But there won't be a next time, will there, Jo?"

Jo smiled sadly. "Probably not. All good things must come to an end. We'll both live." She opened the screen door and stepped through. Before letting it close, she said, "I won't leave without telling you goodbye."

"Thank you. I appreciate that."

As Clary stood helplessly and watched Jo walk briskly across the veranda, she got a sinking feeling in her stomach. It came from the knowledge that if Jo left now, they would never have another opportunity to patch things up between them.

She stepped forward and pushed the screen open again. "Jo?"

Jo stopped and turned around slowly. Her eyes were soft and pleading as she looked at Clary. "Don't, Clary. Don't make this any harder. I can't stand it if we go on this way any longer. Please."

Clary choked back a sob. "Okay. Goodbye, Jo."

"Goodbye."

* * * *

Clary spent the rest of the morning picking up, washing the sheets that Karen had thoughtfully stripped from her bed, and sketching from the veranda. She tried to keep from looking in the direction of Jo's cabin, and it took a conscious effort to keep from brooding about the way they had parted.

About noon, she spotted Jo heading for the lake, fully clothed. Perhaps she wanted to take one last look before leaving. Clary wondered if she'd meant it about saying goodbye. The way things stood, it wouldn't surprise her if Jo disappeared without a word.

After lunch, Clary decided to tackle some of the jobs she'd put off. She'd become adept at maneuvering on the crutches. Getting down to the lake last night had proved that. Now, she felt able to take on some overdue chores. One was to sort through the last of Barbara's belongings, a job she'd put off for too long now. It wasn't going to be pleasant, but it had to be done sometime.

She went to the bedroom, opened the closet, and eyed two boxes on the top shelf. Resting her crutches against the wall, she found that by stretching she could reach them. Carefully, she lifted the first one down and hopped on her good leg with it to the bed. Judging from its weight, the box was full, and she felt a tug in her lower back from the strain of hefting it. She massaged the spot, dismissing the pain. After all, if she paid attention to every little twinge and pull on her middle-aged muscles, she'd be taking pills all the time.

The flaps of the box had been folded in to keep it closed. On one side, Barbara had used a black felt pen to identify the contents. "Hadley family stuff," she'd written in her no-nonsense way.

Inside, Clary found the usual things people save and never look at until their descendants find them and relegate them to a shelf for the next generation. This batch consisted of several yearbooks, family photo albums, awards and certificates, travel posters from Mexico and the Caribbean, dog tags for Hadleys who'd served in the armed forces, dog tags for cherished family pets.

The only things of real interest to Clary were the badges from Barbara's Girl Scout days. She wondered if Barbara's close proximity to all those girls had made up for being barred from the Boy Scouts. She kept the badges out, not sure what she would do with them, replaced the other items, and put the box aside.

The second box was smaller and light enough to remove from the shelf with one hand. No writing designated the contents and several bands of duct tape sealed the lid, as if what were inside was some wonderful secret. She peeled the tape away to find two photo albums and a packet of letters tied together with a faded ribbon.

The plastic pages of the albums had turned brittle with age. It took only a minute to realize that these were not family albums - - no Hadley family portraits, no family outings, no pets. The photos were of Barbara, alone or in a group or, most frequently, with a particular young woman.

The girl had an impish face and mischievous brown eyes. A cleft chin added to her devil-may-care appearance, and a mass of copper hair snaked wildly about her cheeks and curled around her shoulders. Clary imagined it was the kind of hair that would be hell to comb and heaven to bury your fingers in.

The photographs had been arranged in chronological order and, as Clary looked at the dates, she traced a span of eleven years. The last one had been taken on

Barbara's fortieth birthday, a year before Clary had met her.

In the earliest photos, Barbara had worn her hair in a wedge and had gone in for the garish outfits of the times. The other woman seemed always to be nearby, standing with Barbara against a woodsy backdrop, resting an arm on her knee at a party, clowning above the candles on a birthday cake, playing with a rambunctious puppy. Kissing.

The pictures in the second album all seemed to have been taken in the same house. One showed the girl leaning from a ladder over the top of a Christmas tree, her mouth set in determination as she placed the star. Another caught her in the bathtub, bubbles to her chin, bracing the air with her hands in protest at having her picture taken. Pages later, she posed in a red dress, a matching beret cocked at a jaunty angle atop the mass of red-brown hair. Clary knew that Barbara had been the photographer.

Other shots depicted Barbara: reading a book, hunched over her typewriter, washing the car, asleep with her arms thrown in abandon above her head, the sheet barely covering her small breasts. No one except the girl could have taken those.

Clary felt like an intruder in their lives. She also felt incredibly jealous.

She moved the albums to the foot of the bed and picked up the letters, which she knew before she even looked at them had been written to Barbara. She selected one envelope and took out the letter. The paper emitted a faint lilac fragrance as she carefully unfolded it and scanned the first few lines.

Dearest Barbara,

This conference has me bored out of my gourd. Talk, talk, talk! I long for it to be over so I can come home to you. I long for . . .

Without reading further, Clary slid the letter under the ribbon and placed the packet face down on the bottom of the box. Another envelope, bearing no address or postage, lay to one side. Clary removed a yellowed obituary notice.

Riley, Catherine, 35. Died in an automobile accident on May 5. She is survived by her mother and father, Mr. and Mrs. Joseph Riley of Boston, Massachusetts, and by three brothers: Sean, 37, Patrick, 32, and Kyle, 30. Services will be held at St. John of the Cross in San Francisco on May 8 at 2 p.m.

Clary returned the notice to its envelope and put it, along with the two albums, in the box and folded the flaps.
Suddenly, she felt very tired, more tired than she'd ever felt before. She lay back on the bed and covered her eyes with her hands, feeling hot tears flow between her fingers and down her cheeks onto the bed.
Dearest Barbara, she thought, *why didn't you tell me about the girl you loved so well, the girl who returned your love for all those years? Why didn't you share with me the pain you felt when she died? Why didn't you unburden yourself as I longed to do when you were dying?*
She answered her own questions. Barbara hadn't shared because she'd loved Clary, loved her even more perhaps than she'd loved the red-haired girl, because Clary had allowed Barbara to start her life over. The joy of hope had overcome the pain of her loss.
She remembered a passage from Corinthians: "Love is patient, love is kind. It does not envy, it does not boast. It always trusts, always hopes, always perseveres."
It always perseveres.
With an understanding heart, Clary pulled herself upright, dried her tears, and left the room.

Chapter Eighteen

The weather report hadn't mentioned rain, but Clary awoke to a storm more violent than the one that had accompanied her trip from the hospital with Norma. With each crack of thunder, Lucy whined and hunkered into a frightened crouch. The reverberations threatened to break windows, and Clary wondered if she ought to call someone to come tape them over.

Lucy followed sheepishly as she made her way to the kitchen to throw on lights and switch on the radio. The weatherman crooned his report, assuring listeners that the storm was a fluke but admitting he had no idea how long it'd last. He urged them to keep their umbrellas handy and to have their windshield wipers checked, sliding artfully into a commercial for Cal's garage. Knowing Cal, Clary guessed that the air time had probably been bartered for a tune-up.

Making breakfast, she became aware of a twinge in her back. It extended from her waist to her buttocks and throbbed with the slightest movement. Obviously, it had developed when she was removing the boxes with Barbara's belongings from the closet shelves yesterday. Once again, she decided to ignore it, hoping that it would simply get better on its own.

The storm raged on, and Clary contented herself with reading on the sofa, getting up now and then to check for leaks and to look out the window at the maelstrom in the yard. On one such trip, she spotted Jo's Honda still parked beside her cabin, and Clary suspected that her plans to leave had been interrupted by the storm. Even in good weather, driving in the mountains could be tricky. In weather like this, it could be disastrous.

Around one o'clock, Clary resolved to get dressed and find something useful to do. When she pulled her nightgown over her head, stabbing pain shot through her back. She waited for the throbbing to subside and, after some experimentation, found that she could avoid discomfort only by keeping her body ramrod straight.

As the afternoon wore on, her back continued to hurt, even when immobile. By five o'clock, Clary decided that something was definitely wrong and, rain or no rain, she'd better seek medical attention.

Once again, she faced the dilemma of finding someone to drive her to Metcalf.

After gulping down some aspirin, she got on the telephone. No one answered at Cal's garage, which she guessed had been closed because of the storm. Cal wasn't one to hang around and twiddle his thumbs in the absence of business.

She'd barely punched in Norma Latham's number when she heard a knock on the door. The pounding was loud and insistent, probably the last in a series of unsuccessful attempts to be heard above the storm. Clary replaced the receiver and followed Lucy to the door.

Jo stood on the porch soaked to the skin, holding a soggy newspaper above her head as a makeshift umbrella.

"May I come in for a minute?" she asked.

Keeping her body straight, Clary stepped back to admit her. It took their joint effort to close the door against the force of the wind.

Jo smeared water off her cheeks and hair and wiped it on the front of her cotton sweater. "I wouldn't bother you, but it looks as though I'll have to stay over. No driving down the mountain in this storm. I came to pay you for the extra day."

"Don't worry about it. One day's rent won't break me."

But Jo had already pulled the money from the pocket of her khakis. As Clary reached for it, a bolt of pain surged through her back all the way down into her leg. She winced.

"What's wrong?" Jo asked.

"I've done something to my back. It happened when I was moving some boxes yesterday. It's been giving me trouble all day."

Gently, Jo turned Clary around and rubbed the muscles of Clary's lower back. When she came to the affected part, Clary involuntarily let out a cry.

"It's nothing to do with your spine," Jo announced, "but you should definitely have someone look at it. At the very least, the doctor can give you something to take the edge off your pain. Go put on a windbreaker, and I'll drive you over to Metcalf."

In spite of Clary's protests that Metcalf was too far to go in the rain, Jo made her fetch the windbreaker and went to get her car.

Except for a man with an ugly knot on his forehead, they found the emergency room empty. Within minutes, Clary was examined by a doctor who looked as though she belonged in a high school classroom instead of in a hospital emergency room. X-rays were taken just to be sure and, after reading them, the doctor made a diagnosis of muscle strain. For a cure, she recommended hot packs, immobility, anti-inflammatory medication, and a big dose of patience.

Clary sat in the waiting room while Jo took the prescription to the pharmacy and, within the hour, they were back in the Honda headed for home.

Darkness had fallen, and a steady rain pelted the road and ran in sheets down the windshield. Jo put the wipers on high and turned on her brights. They drove without talking, partly because Jo needed quiet to concentrate on the road, but mostly because they'd exhausted their hopes of a truce and had nothing left to say.

As they swung off the main road onto the lake frontage, Clary broke the silence.

"I'm one hell of a mess these days, aren't I? Foot in a cast and now a pulled muscle. At least the back should heal in a few days. The cast seems to be a permanent fixture."

"You definitely count among the disabled," Jo replied.
"I know it seems that the gods have come down hard on you lately, and I haven't made things any easier. I'm sorry. As soon as this storm lifts, I'll get out of here. You can forget all about me, and your life will be back to normal again."

"It would be nice," Clary said slowly, "if we could maintain our friendship. I don't have a lot of people in my life, just the children really, and I'd like it if we could go on as we did before."

Jo slowed to take a curve and turned to look at Clary.

"You know that isn't possible, Clary. My feelings for you go deeper than friendship. They always have. I started to fall in love with you a long time ago, but I kept my feelings to myself because of Barbara. The two of you were so much in love. Even an idiot could see that. I've done some stupid things in my life, but home wrecking was the last thing I wanted to add to the list."

Jo took her eyes off the road momentarily to check Clary's reaction, but Clary's expression remained unreadable. Jo continued, "I thought that maybe after Barbara died . . . " She broke off. "Well, that's water under the bridge now. It's clear that you can't reciprocate what I feel, so it's best for us to make a clean break, don't you agree?"

Clary said nothing.

The road to the house had become a river. The car slid precariously in the mud, and Jo put a white-knuckle grip on the wheel to keep them from ending up in a ditch. As they approached the house, they could hear Lucy barking. From her window, Clary could see the dog crouched in an attack stance at the top of the steps.

"What's Lucy doing outside?" she asked rhetorically. "Either I left the door open or she's gone out the pantry window again. Guess I'll have to nail it shut to keep her in."

Jo cut the engine and sighed with dread, Clary thought, at the prospect of getting her invalid charge into the house in the downpour. Her ability to maneuver had been limited enough with the crutches. Now, with her wrenched back, it would be twice as hard.

"It's a sure bet we won't come out of this with dry underwear," Jo said. "Are you ready?"

"As ready as I'll ever be."

Jo flung open her door, hurried around the car, and took the crutches out. Clary scooted to the edge of the seat and carefully set her good foot down in the mud, trying not to twist her torso in the process. Lucy continued to bark as Jo positioned the crutches and helped Clary step away so the door could be closed. Driving rain assaulted them, shooting needles of water into their faces. The rubber foot of a crutch slipped out from under Clary, sending her wildly off balance. She grabbed frantically for Jo.

"Shut up, Lucy!" she shouted in her frustration.

The dog ventured down the steps, head hung low, whining softly.

Supporting Clary by an elbow, Jo leaned down, retrieved the crutch, and kept it in hand, encircling Clary's waist firmly with her other arm.

"Stay close to me and see if you can make it on one leg. I won't let you fall."

Somehow, the two managed to struggle up the steps to the veranda. Under the shield of its roof, they stopped to rest before proceeding to the door. If it had been left open, the wind had sucked it shut again.

As Clary pulled open the screen, Lucy edged in front of her, pressing her nose to the crack nervously. Clary nudged her out of the way.

"I don't know what's gotten into her," she said to Jo. "She's never acted this way before, not even in worse storms than this."

Jo reached over her head and pushed the door open, but before they could go through, Lucy plunged ahead and began dashing wildly about the living room. Inside, it was dark as the bottom of a well. Clary inched across the threshold and stopped a few feet in.

"There's a lamp on that table by the sofa," she told Jo. "Be careful of the throw rugs."

Suddenly, a gust of wind slammed the door shut, and they were left with only the sound of the banging screen. Lucy continued to scurry from corner to corner. She'd ceased barking, and only the sound of her panting and her toenails clicking on the hardwood floor told them her whereabouts.

Clary could barely see Jo, who was standing in the center of the room, not moving. She wondered what kept her from going to turn on the lamp. Perhaps she hadn't understood which table.

"It's to the left of the - -"

Jo cut her off. "Quiet. Listen."

An eerie sound, like the chirping of tiny birds, only sharper and more rapid, filled the room. Clary had heard the sound before, but she couldn't place it. Underneath the chirping, she detected a scratching sound, like twigs being dragged across sandpaper.

As her eyes adjusted to the dark, a blur of movement at her feet made her gasp. She could make out single dartings, hordes on the run, skittering under the chairs and hovering in the corners. And now she saw eyes, small red pinheads, glinting in the darkness.

"What is it?" she whispered to Jo, her voice raspy with fear.

"Rats," Jo said. She spoke as calmly as if she were announcing the time of day.

Clary pulled in a breath so strong it felt like rocks pelting her breastbone. She released it in a moan. Her hand flew to her chest in an effort to quell the thudding of her heart against her ribs. At her feet, a pack of the dark creatures scurried past, chittering their birdlike sound.

Lucy darted after them, knocking a crutch out from under her.

It fell to the floor, and Clary went down. The force of her fall sent her sprawling, and her head slammed into the floor. Instinctively, she struggled upright and tried to get to her feet, but she found the task impossible.

She could see the rats gathering like vultures around a kill. Up close, she could see their red eyes, the twitching of their whiskers, their oily fur.

Jo's voice came from the end of a long, dark tunnel. "Are you all right?"

"I think so," she managed.

"Stay where you are. They won't hurt you. I'm going for the lights."

Claws bit into the skin of Clary's hand as the rats ran over her. She pulled the hand away, crossed her arms over her chest, and pulled her legs into a fetal position. "Hurry," she moaned.

Jo managed to find the lamp and turn it on. As Clary reached out to Jo, a wave of black overtook her, and she lapsed into unconsciousness.

Chapter Nineteen

Clary awoke in a chair on the veranda, feeling like a drunk who'd suddenly come to in a strange bed. Lucy watched her with big eyes, while Jo stood by anxiously, her fingers playing nervously about her mouth.

Her voice was fraught with concern. "Talk to me, Clary. I need to know that your brain is still intact after that fall."

Clary remembered going down and fingered the bump on her head. "How'd I get out here?"

"I carried you. Somehow, I didn't think it was a good idea to let you regain consciousness among our furry friends. They're locked inside for the night. You'll stay with me. Can you make it to the cabin?"

Clary realized she was shaking and that the lump on the back of her skull had begun to throb, as had her wrenched back. Getting herself back in the car for the ride down to Telluride seemed a gargantuan task, but obviously she couldn't sit here all night.

She struggled to her feet and stood for a moment, testing her balance. Jo helped her into her crutches and encircled her waist as they moved tentatively across the veranda and descended the steps.

The rain had abated, but dark clouds still cloaked the sky, and the air felt heavy. Jo helped Clary get to the car and, slowly, to avoid jarring her back, drove down the hill. At one point, a wave of blackness threatened and Jo stopped the car to cradle Clary's head against her shoulder until it passed.

On the porch, Jo unlocked her door, glancing at Clary to be sure she was all right. Clary stood shivering, plagued by the feeling that she was a participant in some crazy dream. Vaguely she wondered about the blow to her head and said the days of the week under her breath.

Gently, Jo pushed her across the threshold, and Clary heard the door shut and the click of the lock behind them. She knew that Jo was talking, but the words were a scramble of nonsense. Pressure against her back coincided with "Come over here," and she allowed herself to be pushed across the room and deposited in a chair.

Jo switched on a lamp and scrutinized Clary's face.

"You're not going to pass out on me again, are you?"

"I'm not sure. Don't go away."

She pulled her knees up under her chin and fought to monitor her breathing as the lingering terror of the rats continued to rock her.

Jo stood, grazing her forehead with helpless fingers, tilting her head in concern as she studied Clary's face in the diffuse light.

"It's over now," she said. "Try to stop thinking about it."

But Clary couldn't stop. The vision of the rats reverberated in her mind, like a horror scene in a movie. She fought to keep from crying, but when she could no longer stifle the sobs, she lowered her head to her knees and let them go.

Jo brought a blanket, which she draped loosely around Clary, who pulled it close, clutching it to her throat, twining her legs in the folds. She could hear Jo in the kitchen opening cupboards, then liquid being poured into glasses. Jo came back and held one out with the seriousness of a parent offering medicine to a child.

"It's brandy," she said. "Take it in one swallow."

Dutifully, Clary downed the alcohol, feeling it ignite her throat. Jo took hers to the sofa and watched anxiously over the rim of her glass. It felt to Clary like a time in the third grade when a baseball had split her lip and the people in the nurse's office had stood staring at her as if she'd just climbed out of a space ship.

"I'm all right," she told Jo. "You don't have to stay with me. The sofa makes up into a bed. I'll be fine."

Jo went to the bedroom, returning with a nightgown and a pillow. The nightgown looked blue, but in the dim light it might have been any color. She lay the pillow in a chair and offered the gown by one strap.

"It'll be too big, but I doubt you care right now."

"I don't."

Jo took sheets from the cupboard and made up the bed.

When she'd finished, she said, "It's not a suite at the Ritz, but it'll do. You need to get some sleep."

"Thank you."

Jo went into the bedroom and closed the door.

Clary unfurled from her blanket, undressed, and struggled into the nightgown. She laid her crutches on the floor and spread the blanket haphazardly across the mattress. In bed, she felt the urge to cry again, but even crying takes energy, and hers had all been drained away. Exhausted, she gave in to sleep, which swept over her like fog over the lake in winter.

She didn't know if she'd slept for minutes or hours when a sound awakened her. She shot upright, listening for the source, only to realize that it was a cry and that the cry had come from her own throat. She waited to see if there would be another, as if her terror had a life of its own. She heard only rain and the slap of a window shade in the breeze through a slightly open window. She eased onto her back and stared into the darkness.

"Clary, what's wrong?" Jo was standing in the doorway.

"I must have been dreaming. I didn't mean to wake you."

Jo crossed the room and stood over the sofa bed, staring down like the people in the nurse's office. Clary raised a hand to ward off her concern, but Jo ignored it and sat on the edge of the bed.

"You've been moaning in your sleep all night. I wanted to come comfort you but . . . "

"I wish you had," Clary said quickly.

Jo angled in beside her and rested her cheek against Clary's hair, then hesitantly enveloped her in an embrace. Slowly, she rocked, stroking and crooning words of comfort. Clary curled in and yielded to the reassurance of her caring.

They sat like that for several minutes, bodies pressed together in a mutual dance of compassion. Then, as suddenly as it had begun, the dance slowed, the stroking stopped, and Clary felt emptiness where Jo had been. She opened her eyes to see Jo's long back at the edge of the bed, a barricade against intimacy.

"Why did you stop?" Clary whispered.

"I think I should go back to my own room. This is making me . . . "

Clary grasped Jo's shoulder, turning her until they faced. Jo started to speak, but before she could, Clary had pulled her body close. Her lips found Jo's throat and pulsed to her pulse. The throb of life beneath her mouth was incredibly arousing. She moved her tongue over the curve of Jo's throat to the valley at the base, then back to find her mouth. Jo's lips parted to admit her, and Clary explored, tasting the bittersweetness of brandy.

She untied the sash of Jo's robe and parted the fabric. Underneath, Jo was naked. She trailed her fingers across Jo's abdomen to her thigh, down inside and slowly up again, brushing the soft triangle of hair. Jo's skin was smooth, stretched silk as Clary's fingers traveled to her full breasts.

Suddenly, Jo jerked away and clamped down on Clary's wrist, anchoring it to the mattress. Her breath came in frantic bursts.

"We can't do this. You're confusing your need for comfort with desire. You'll blame me afterward, or you'll blame yourself."

Clary pulled her wrist free and fell back on the bed, stretching her arms above her head. Jo's gown failed to cover her breasts, and Jo stared at them unabashedly. Clary resisted the urge to pull Jo's head down to nestle on her fullness. She knew they had to talk.

She sat up and engaged Jo's eyes. "I went through some of Barbara's things yesterday. What I found changed the way
I feel about you." She paused. "No, that's not it. They allowed me to be honest about feelings I didn't want to admit."

"I don't understand."

Clary ran her fingers through her hair, then covered her mouth as if to contain her words until she had them set.

"Barbara had some photo albums I'd never seen before. They contained pictures of a lover I hadn't known existed. They were together for eleven years before the girl died. At first, I felt jealous and angry. Then, I realized why Barbara had shielded me. She understood that love is not exclusive, that a person can have more than one love in her life. Barbara's gone now. I will always love her. But she showed me, even in her death, that I have the right to love again." She reached out to touch Jo's cheek. "I want to love you."

Jo questioned with her eyes, looking into Clary's for a long time. When Clary smiled and leaned to brush Jo's mouth with hers, Jo yielded and took her in.

They had nothing more to talk about.

Her mouth still engaged, Jo turned Clary and lowered her onto her back, blanketing her body along one side. She explored with her fingers, passionate and slow. When she took her mouth away and tongued her way to Clary's breast, her desire came fast, and the fire ignited them both.

Quickly, Jo sat up and slid out of her robe, dropping it over the side of the bed. She balanced on her knees and eased the ill-fitting gown off Clary's shoulders, her fingers grazing Clary's skin as she pulled the garment to her waist. She waited for Clary to raise her hips, then slid it off and tossed it away to join the abandoned robe. Pulling upright, Jo arched her back, offering her breasts for Clary to cup and stroke, her nipples growing hard with each pass of Clary's thumb.

Clary lay back and freed her mind, closed her eyes, opened her senses. Jo nestled beside her, her body soft and warm. Jo teased with her tongue, running it over the fullness of Clary's breast, pulling it over her nipple, moving to Clary's throat, pressing in, stroking in sync with her heartbeat.

She put her mouth to Clary's ear. "I'll stop now. If you want to change your mind, I promise I will stop."

In response, Clary took Jo's head between her hands, guided Jo's mouth to her other breast. Jo's mouth stayed there for a long time, the palm of her hand pulsing rhythmically on Clary's abdomen, coaxing the desire within, fingers pulling gently through the hair beneath. Clary's hips rose with her urgency. A gentle wave of release swept her body and slid softly through.

Jo pushed upright, looked at her and smiled. In the half darkness, Clary met her gaze and smiled back. Jo's eyes were darker than the swimming pool the other night.

"It's been a long time for you, hasn't it?" Jo said.

"Longer than I can remember. I'm afraid I've become easy." She reached to circle one of Jo's nipples with the tips of her fingers. "Make it easy for me again."

Slowly, Jo tried Clary's mouth, exploring with her tongue until both their breaths had gone. And then she stopped, gasping for air like a person drowning.

Clary moved her hands down the length of Jo's body, inching into the warm pool between her thighs. Jo moved her hand away.

"No fair," she said. "You have to let me finish what I've started. You say you're easy. Let me find out."

Deftly, she maneuvered to the foot of the bed, grazed the instep of Clary's foot with soft lips, caressed with her tongue, came up the length of her calf, and paused inside her thigh. Clary closed her fists on Jo's hair and guided her mouth to the place of her wanting. Parting her legs, she drew Jo down onto her, frantic for relief from her exquisite desire.

"Please," she begged. "Now, please."

Jo's hands worked along her sides, her tongue firm on Clary's growing hardness. This time, the waves came frantic and fast until Clary cried out from the ecstasy, her ripe release mixing inexorably with her joy. Again and again, she responded to Jo's urgent loving, shudders of pleasure racking her body.

Finally spent, she lay back and pulled Jo to her, on top of her, luxuriating in the softness of their cushioned breasts, their intertwined legs. She breathed into Jo's hair, nuzzled an ear, ran her fingers the length of Jo's long back. Waves of lingering ecstasy passed through her body like ripples on the lake.

When she'd regained herself, Clary breathed, "This cast makes it hard. I want to love you as you've loved me, but I don't know if I can."

Jo lay motionless, and Clary knew she was reveling in her power. Somehow, she sensed that Jo wasn't used to others loving her. She was the lover. She was in control.

Without a word, Jo rolled away and sat on the edge of the bed, her knees pulled up under her chin. Her pale breasts touched her thighs, her head rested on her knees.

"Loving you was enough."

But it wasn't enough for Clary. Taking Jo's head between her hands, she kissed her and pushed her onto her back, fighting Jo's resistance.

"Let me," Clary said. "I'll feel cheated if you don't."

Jo smiled. "I certainly wouldn't want you to feel cheated. I always pride myself on playing fair."

Slowly, Clary bathed Jo's skin with her tongue, sliding her fingers across the wet trail. She pushed her body to the end of the bed, dragging the cast, and parted Jo's thighs. Jo gave in until she lay open like a flower. Clary caressed the blossom with her mouth, savoring the silky wetness. She stroked softly at first, then harder and deeper, reveling in the way Jo's hips pulsed and thrust. She left her on the brink of release and moved up, replacing her lips with fingers.

Head thrust back, arms outstretched, Jo writhed, longing for completion. She covered Clary's hand with her own, pressed her fingers in harder, stroking Clary's hand to set the tempo for release. When Clary entered her, the orgasm came, awesome in its strength. Jo's pulse beat around Clary's fingers, and she kept them inside, relishing the sheer force and joy of the magnificent contractions.

When Jo's desire was spent, she pulled Clary's hand across her body, trailing liquid love to the nipple of one breast. Clary circled with a finger, rested her head on Jo's abdomen, breathed in time to Jo's breathing.

Outside on the porch, Lucy whined.

"Shall we let her in?" Clary asked.

"Not yet. I need to come down to earth."

Clary found the tangle of sheet at the foot of the bed and pulled it up to cover Jo. "I think I love you," she said.
"I did my best to keep myself from knowing, but now I do."
It was the closest she'd come to the truth in a long time.
I think," Jo said, "that I've always loved you."

Chapter Twenty

It rained on and off for the remainder of the night, and Clary slept fitfully. Once, she experienced another nightmare, less intense than the one before but still frightening. This time, Jo was beside her, spooning into her back, encouraging her to forget.

They made love again sometime before dawn, a soft, sweeping-in of gentle caresses and easy kisses very different from their earlier hungry energy. Afterward, while Jo slept, Clary watched the morning make itself known through the open window. The wind had died to a whisper, and birds sang into the silence, announcing the new day.

Beside her, Jo stirred and opened her eyes. Confusion etched her face as she struggled to recognize the strange room, the strange bed and, perhaps, even the stranger who lay beside her. When she did, she reached from beneath the sheets and touched Clary's lips.

"Do you feel strong?" she asked.

Laughing, Clary took Jo's hand and cushioned it against her breast. "You are dealing with a forty-two-year-old woman here, not Sheena of the jungle, you know."

Jo smiled. "I just thought, if you were in the mood."

"Much as I'd like to be ravished again, I'll have to pass. Lucy is probably starving, and I need to do something about those rats." She cringed as she said the word. "Guess I'll have to get an exterminator."

"An exterminator is definitely in order, that is, unless you intend to go in with a broom and shoo them out. Let's have breakfast, then we'll work on it. But first . . ."

She grabbed Clary by the back of the neck and pulled her into an open-mouthed kiss, pinning her with an arm.

Clary submitted for a minute, then pulled away. "Jo, let go of me so I can get with the program."

Jo released her arm and pulled back to look at her. "Pretty bossy, aren't you?"

Clary sat up gingerly and lowered her casted leg to the floor. "I didn't mean to sound that way. It's just that I have things to do."

Jo smiled. "You can be as bossy as you like, as long as you jump my bones at least once a day, or night, or both." She sobered. "You really are a marvelous lover, you know."

"I didn't know, but it's nice to hear."

"I'd be happy to reaffirm it - - every time I get the chance."

They made up the sofa and launched into cold cereal, which, in the absence of her regular food, Lucy seemed to enjoy as much as they did.

After breakfast, Jo showered and dressed and sat down with the yellow pages while Clary took a sponge bath, silently cursing her cast. From the bathroom, she could hear Jo talking to exterminators on the phone. When she emerged, Jo announced that she'd engaged an outfit named Bug Busters who'd assured her they could handle an infestation of rodents as well as they could handle ants. They'd be here soon to set the traps and, with luck, the rats would be dead by tomorrow morning.

"I'm afraid to ask," Clary said, "but what's the going rate for zapping a houseful of rats these days?"

"Six hundred dollars."

Clary winced. "These pranks are not only scaring me to death, they're breaking me. Frankly, Jo, I don't know how I'm going to handle the debt. Six hundred dollars for this, seven hundred for de-flooding the house, two fifty for cleaning up the remains of the shed, not to mention the down payment Richard needs for the garage. Short of declaring bankruptcy, I have no idea what I'm going to do."

"I've been thinking about that," Jo said quietly. She paced the room, stopping at the window to stare out. "I hat to say this, Clary, but I think your options have run out. You need to sell this place and not only because you need the money. You simply cannot hang around waiting for the next catastrophe. After last night, I'm convinced that the twisted mind who wants you out will stop at nothing. I don't want to scare you, but I think your life could be in jeopardy."

"I agree with you," Clary said. "As much as I dislike Kahn, it looks as if I'm going to have to sell to him after all. There's a very good chance that he's the one who's been harassing me in the hopes of scaring me into it, either him or his henchman. I'd hate to think it was any of my neighbors, but it doesn't matter now. They'll be happy, Kahn will be happy, everyone except me will be happy."

"You'll miss this place, won't you?"

"More than anyone knows. But life goes on, as they say. And, speaking of life going on, if it hadn't been for the storm and those rats, you'd be back in Santa Rosa getting on with yours right now."

Jo bent down to nuzzle her ear. "I could have skipped the storm and the rats, but I wouldn't have missed last night for anything. I'd like for there to be a lot more nights like that and days and months and years and - - "

"Forever?"

"Yes, forever. What are we . . . ?"

Clary touched her fingers to Jo's lips to silence her.

"It's too soon, Jo. I just can't think about it now. So much has happened. I need time."

Jo took her hand away and kissed the palm. "I understand. When are you going to contact Kahn?"

"Today, after you leave."

"The exterminators said it'd take twenty-four hours for our little friends to give up the ghost, which means you can't sleep in your house tonight. I hate to think of you all alone down in this cabin. Maybe I should stay another day and keep you company?"

"I'd love that."

"Done then. For dinner tonight, how about repeating the lakeshore picnic you had with Karen? Mind revving up the hibachi again?"

"Not if you do the revving. This foot makes me useless. What do you feel like eating?"

Jo adopted a mischievous expression. "Something exotic. Broiled squid and artichoke hearts? Marinated sweet breads with caesar salad? Pork chops and chocolate ice cream?"

Clary leaned into Jo, laughing. "How about good old American hot dogs with mustard and plenty of chopped red onions? And for dessert, Oreo cookies. Exotic enough for you?"

"Perfect."

They watched for the exterminators and drove up the hill to meet them when they arrived. Clary stayed in the Honda while Jo explained the situation. The thought of being near the house still filled her with terror, and she wondered if she'd be able to go inside even after the creatures had been removed.

As soon as the men had begun their tasks, they went into town for groceries. Marissa came out of her cabin as they headed up the drive, her eyes on the ground in an effort to avoid stepping in the gullies left by the storm. Now and then, her mouth moved and, although they couldn't hear her words, it was a sure bet she wasn't praising Mother Nature for the bountiful rain.

Jo pulled the car beside her and stopped. "We're on our way into town. Want a lift to the Inn?"

"Why not? These shoes were too expensive to have them fucked up with mud."

Jo reached around and unlocked the back door. "Nothing worse than fucked-up shoes, is there?"

Clary stifled a guffaw. Marissa frowned, unsure how to take Jo's remark. "Damn right," she said finally.

Unlikely as it seemed, Clary considered the possibility that Marissa had released the rats. It had probably taken a vehicle to transport the rodents from a lab, or wherever they'd come from, and Marissa had no car. Still, Clary decided to test the winds.

She turned around in her seat in order to see Marissa's face. "Know much about rodents?"

The girl failed to show the slightest flicker of emotion. "You mean like hamsters or mice? Like that?"

"Or like rats."

Marissa shrugged. "Why should I know anything about rats? Unless you mean the human kind. I've had a couple of boyfriends who'd qualify, if you know what I mean."

Clary smiled. "I can imagine."

"Yeah, I guess you'd have to. Imagine, I mean. You sure wouldn't know about boyfriends."

Clary was about to explode when she caught an admonishing look from Jo. She held her tongue and faced front as they drove the rest of the way to the Inn.

In the parking lot, Marissa jumped out and hurried to the door, muttering her thanks.

After she disappeared inside, Clary remarked, "I suppose the last thing she wants is to be seen in the company of two dykes."

"The last thing I want is to be seen in the company of a teenybopper with the vocabulary of an elementary school dropout, you know what I mean?"

Jo slurred the words to imitate Marissa, and Clary laughed.

"Good thing you were in the car. I was on the verge of belting her over that remark about boyfriends."

"Just remember who you're dealing with. It isn't worth the effort to try and get back."

"You're right."

After their errands, they spent the rest of the morning lazing about, reading and sitting in the sun.

Late in the afternoon, Jo decided to take a swim, and Clary announced that she could use a nap. After the emotional upheaval of the previous night, she felt as if she could sleep forever. They parted, savoring the separation because of the sweet knowledge of their coming together again.

As Clary settled into Jo's big double bed, her heart sang with a happiness she had thought she'd never feel again. She quickly fell into a dreamless sleep and awoke to find Jo leaning over the bed in her bathing suit, dripping water onto the carpet.

"Get up, sleepy head. You've slept forever. Let's go cook those hot dogs."

Jo changed out of her wet bathing suit and lugged the hibachi down the hill with Clary and Lucy following. They settled in nearly the same spot Clary and Karen had occupied just days before.

Clary stood on her crutches, watching Jo tend to the coals as the setting sun cast a pink glow over the lake and spread magical color through the leaves of the oak trees. Jo's face was lit with magic, too, whether from the glow of the fire or from her newfound happiness, Clary couldn't tell. She preferred to attribute it to happiness. If only Karen could see them. She'd be so pleased to know that the love Clary had been denying herself was finally coming to fruition.

They ate their fill of hot dogs, dripping mustard on the blanket and on their clothes and not caring. Lucy got her share too, and Clary worried out loud about her digestive system.

"Good Lord, Clary," Jo said, "If the old girl can survive a dose of snail bait, she can certainly survive a couple of hot dogs."

Clary impulsively fed her another one.

As the sun descended below the horizon, Jo settled beside Clary on the blanket, waiting for the coals to die down. Clary felt a magnetism as strong as any she'd felt with Barbara. As the electricity grew, she couldn't keep herself from reaching out to touch Jo's face, tracing the outline of her strong cheekbones, following the curve of her throat to the opening of her shirt. Jo's breast felt heavy under her searching fingers.

"Shall we pack up and go home to that bed we talked about?" Clary asked.

"Let's stay here. I can't think of a more appropriate place to make love than beside this beautiful lake."

Quickly, Jo rose to her knees and pulled her shirt over her head, then removed Clary's tank top.

"Glad to see that we're both liberated enough to dispense with bras in this weather," she said. "I've been sneaking peeks at your liberation all day."

"As I have at yours," Clary admitted.

Jo came softly, cushioning her breasts against Clary's, nuzzling her neck. Her tongue moved down Clary's chest to the nipple of one breast. Jo suckled and bit as her desire mounted.

Jo's unzipped Clary's jeans and then pressed her knuckles against the crotch of Clary's panties.

"I see you're only halfway liberated," Jo breathed.

Her fingers edged under the elastic, inching deftly into Clary's wetness, stroking slowly. With her free hand, she cupped a breast and teased a nipple into erectness, kissing softly in rhythm with her strokes. Clary's hips rose, thrust, lowered, and thrust again, moving faster as Jo increased her tempo, her body an instrument being played at Jo's discretion. She wanted the song to last forever.

Suddenly, Jo stopped moving and covered Clary's body with hers, withholding what was needed to put her over the edge.

"God, don't stop now," Clary gasped.

Propping herself on one elbow, Jo watched Clary's face and rested the palm of her hand on Clary's crotch, not moving. She pressed the knuckle of her thumb down firmly, holding it steady. Clary's hips rose one last time and held as she writhed against Jo's hand. Her climax spread in rolling waves, and she bit the back of her own hand to muffle her moans. At last, she lay back, pulling in long breaths.

Jo watched her, a satisfied smile playing on her lips.

"You hardly make me work at all," she said.

"That's because I've practically become a virgin," Clary breathed. "This lake isn't exactly overflowing with available women. And you, my darling, could bat your eyelashes at me and I'd come."

She reached up and ran her hand, fingers spread, over the pale nipples of Jo's breasts, watching them peak under her caresses. Jo swiveled to straddle her, bracing herself with locked elbows, bending to let Clary taste her nipples. Clary's mouth captured and held one breast, then repeated on the other side. She hooked one thumb in the waistband of Jo's shorts.

"Take these off. I want to taste you all over."

Jo stood up and pulled the shorts over her slim hips, kicking them away before she knelt again. She arched her back and slid her hands down the length of her own body, knowing, Clary realized, the pleasure it gave Clary to watch. Clary joined Jo in her caressing, luxuriating in that smooth, pale skin. When she stirred to get up, Jo pinned her gently to the blanket.

"Stay. I like you on your back. Besides, it's better for that broken foot if you don't flail it around. I'll make the tasting easy for you."

And she did, straddling Clary's face, presenting herself in open wanting, parting her own lips to leave Clary's hands free to stroke and caress. Her ecstasy expressed itself in throaty moans and wanton urgings. When release finally came, she emitted a series of sharp cries, rending the summer air with her satisfaction.

Spent, she removed Clary's hands from her hips and fell on the blanket, her breath coming in shudders.

"Do you always make your partners see stars?" she asked, when she was able to speak.

The question took Clary aback, and she remained silent, hoping Jo wouldn't press for an answer.

"Do you?" Jo persisted.

"I was with Barbara for so long, I don't remember much before that. Even after all the years we were together, she was still aroused by a touch. So was I."

Jo touched her arm, concern filling her eyes. "I'm sorry. I forgot that you two spent so many years together. Frankly, I've had so many short-lived romances, I'd nearly forgotten
that there are long-standing couples in the world."

Jo lay back and fixed her gaze on the sky, which had begun to dot with stars. "It must be marvelous to have someone, the same someone, react so powerfully. It must make you feel very safe."

"It did," Clary replied. "Funny thing is, I feel just as safe with you."

Jo smiled and kissed her quickly. "I'm glad."

Soon, they began their trek back to Jo's cabin, Jo carried as much as she could, then made a second trip for the remainder.

"You see?" she teased Clary as she put the leftovers in the refrigerator. "Your love making has sapped my strength. You've turned me into a weakling."

"That's good," Clary rejoined. "Perhaps it'll keep you on your own side of the bed tonight. I told you this morning, Sheena of the jungle, I'm not. Once a day is about all I can handle."

Jo winked. "We'll see."

With nothing decent to watch on television, Jo read out loud to Clary from her novel. They ate Oreo cookies and avoided talking about the calories. No sense in spoiling a perfectly lovely dessert.

Around ten, they decided to go to bed. Clary undressed but Jo stopped her from climbing into the borrowed nightgown.

"It fits you like a gunnysack. You'll just wiggle out of it in your sleep," she reasoned. "Besides, this way I'll get to feel you naked against me all night."

"As long as it doesn't involve hands, we'll be all right," Clary said.

In bed, arms entwined, bathed in the light of the moon from the open window, Jo asked, "Have you decided where you'll go after you sell this place?"

"I don't have too many options, not unless I want to live alone in a strange city. I've always liked San Francisco, and Karen's there. Maybe I'll get a place near the water. It won't be the lake, but I can pretend."

"And when Karen takes a job in New York or Timbuktu? What then?"

The thought had entered Clary's mind more than once, but she didn't want to deal with it. "I'll cross that bridge when I come to it."

Jo shifted and turned to Clary. "What about Santa Rosa?" she asked.

"I'd feel more at home in Timbuktu. There's nothing in Santa Rosa to attract me," she said.

Now, Jo did touch her, brushing her fingertips down one side, making circles on her abdomen under the sheet. "I seem to attract you, and I live in Santa Rosa. Love thrives there. Would you come live with me?"

The question seemed to come out of the blue, but Clary knew better. Jo wasn't the sort of person to make offers like that without a good deal of thought. Clary was surprised that Jo felt their relationship had progressed to that point. They'd become lovers but, in Clary's mind, that was only a beginning. Not that she counted herself among the short-lived romances Jo had mentioned earlier, but living with anyone besides Barbara hadn't even crossed her mind. She couldn't fathom sharing her life with anyone else.

She kissed Jo's lips. "Dear Jo. I appreciate your offer. I'm flattered that you think enough of me to invite me into your life, but it simply wouldn't work right now."

Jo turned away. "I've always had this funny idea that when two people are attracted to one another, it's natural for them to share their lives in a permanent way."

The bitterness in her voice alarmed Clary. From Jo's reaction, it seemed clear that she had marshaled her defenses in advance.

"I have two reasons, Jo. First, it's much too soon for us to make that kind of commitment. In six months or a year,
we'll know better. You have to allow us time to find out if this is just physical attraction or if there's more to it."

"As far as I'm concerned, there's more to it. It's not because of Barbara anymore, is it?" Jo asked.

"No. Now, it's just because of me. I don't want to be unfair to you, and I don't want to be unfair to myself. It would be disastrous if we rearranged our lives only to discover that you're a night person and I'm a morning person or something. Besides, what would I do with Lucy?"

"Bring her, of course. I don't have a lake for her to swim in, but I do have a yard, and there's a park two blocks away. As far as night people and morning people, we could make up for it in the middle of the day. I adore making love in broad daylight. What else?"

"The difference in our ages. A lot of living goes on in twelve years -- not that I'd leave you in the dust with my worldly experience. It's simply too large a gap."

"It might be if I were seventeen and you were twenty-nine, but at this point, what difference does it make?"

Before Clary could reply, Jo asked, "How much older was Barbara than you?"

Clary swallowed. "Nine years."

"That relationship worked out."

"Yes."

"But you think it was the exception?"

"Yes."

"The world is full of exceptions."

"I suppose."

"You and I could be an exception too."

"Yes."

Jo pressed into Clary's body and whispered in her ear. "Now that you're on a roll of yesses, answer this. Do you want to make love again, Sheena of the jungle?"

Without hesitation, Clary answered, "Yes."

Chapter Twenty-one

The next morning, Clary and Jo stayed in bed well after they'd both awakened, prolonging their time together before Jo went home.

In the kitchen, as Clary made coffee, Jo came to stand behind her, massaging her neck and running her fingers through Clary's hair.

"Come and begin a new life with me," she whispered into Clary's ear.

"Oh Jo, I can't just - - " Her words were stifled by Jo's kiss.

When the kiss ended, Jo encircled Clary's waist. "Someone said it before, but it seems apropos. Come live with me and be my love."

Clary closed her eyes, racked with indecision. When she started to speak, Jo kissed her again, this time with a longing that tore at her soul.

"Please come."

Clary remembered Barbara's photo album and the red-haired girl, and she thought of the life she and Barbara had shared, the life she and Jo could share if only she could find it in herself to give in.

With Jo's kiss still warm on her mouth and her loving arms around Clary's body, giving in came easier than she thought possible.

"All right. Yes."

Jo pushed back and stared at her, eyes bright with excitement. "Do you mean it? You'll come to Santa Rosa with me?"

Clary reached to stroke Jo's cheek. "I owe it to you to find out if you're right."

"About what?"

"About Santa Rosa being a city where love thrives."

Jo captured her hand and kissed the palm. "I promise you won't be disappointed."

For the next hour, Jo expressed her joy by cooking and talking nonstop. Scrambling the eggs, she explored the possibilities of their new life together. She'd enclose the patio so that Clary could paint out there, put in a spa, build a dog house for Lucy. Clary wouldn't have to do anything, she said, except walk the dog and paint. Life would be fresh and exciting and wonderful. In spite of her reservations about their moving in together so soon, Clary was caught up in Jo's exuberance, and she found herself singing while she dressed. With their love for one another, they could overcome any obstacle.

Buttoning her shirt, Clary looked down at her hands and was suddenly aware of Barbara's ring. Rarely had she removed it since the day Barbara had placed it on her finger. Now, she slid it off and put it in her pocket, intending to transfer it to her jewelry box when she got home. The part of her life she had spent with Barbara was over; she would always remember it, even without the ring to remind her. Now, it was time to move on, to move on to her new life with Jo.

The exterminators arrived around eight to remove the traps, and Jo accompanied Clary to the house to pay them. She felt certain the check would bounce but, as soon as she made her deal with Kahn, her troubles would be over. She'd have enough money to pay every penny of debt she'd accrued.

In the yard, Clary said, "I know I can move back into my house now, but could I stay in Telluride with you tonight? I'm still not over those awful rats. I'd be dreaming about them all night."

Jo frowned. "Oh darling, of course you can stay in the cabin, only it'll have to be without me. I need to take care of some things at home, including rearranging my house to accommodate two. Plus, you need time alone to work out your deal with Kahn. I'll think about you every minute we're apart and, as soon as you're ready, I'll come back to help you pack."

Clary felt less than thrilled at the prospect of being without Jo, but she was right. They'd have plenty of time to be together after the sale of the property was finalized. With luck, they'd have the rest of their lives.

Before leaving, Jo walked Clary through the house, humoring her by checking under the beds and in drawers to confirm the absence of any rats. There was still plenty of evidence left behind, droppings on the floor and in the cupboards. She could take care of that. Just as long as she didn't have to face the horrible creatures in person, she'd be okay.

When Clary felt comfortable, Jo put her Honda in gear, promised to call that evening, and left for home.

To stave off her loneliness, Clary dialed Karen's number in San Francisco. Trying to keep her exuberance under control, she told her about her decision to sell her property and about her new relationship with Jo.

When Karen heard, she let out a whoop that could probably be heard all the way to Sacramento. "I just knew you had the hots for each other," Karen said.

"Karen!" Clary protested.

"Well, you do, don't you? You are going to be so good together. How long did she have to twist your arm before you agreed to go live with her?"

"Three whole nights. Two in a bed, one down at the lake on a blanket," she laughed.

"I am so glad for you, Mom. You deserve every good thing that happens to you."

It was only after she'd hung up that Clary noticed the light on her message machine blinking. The tape contained a lengthy message from Doris Matthews outlining her mother's recovery and announcing that she'd come for Marissa that afternoon. As Clary erased the message, she realized that she hadn't given Marissa a thought in days. The fact that she'd gone unnoticed was a good sign. At least, she'd stayed out of trouble. Clary didn't waste any time getting into her crutches for the trek down to Tahoe to tell Marissa about her mother's arrival.

Marissa came to the door with a can of Diet Coke in one hand and a cigarette in the other. "Want to come in? See if I have anyone hidden under the bed?"

Clary ignored her. "Your mother phoned last night and left a message. Your grandmother's better, and Doris is coming for you this afternoon. You'll need to tell Ellen that you won't be working after today."

The girl took a drag on her cigarette. "Cool. It was starting to look like I'd have to spend the whole damned summer here. What time's she coming?"

"She didn't say. You should probably be back by noon."

Marissa flicked the cigarette out the door into the dirt. "About all I have to do is pack. Not too many goodbyes to say. Dale's the only person I'm going to miss around here."

The inference was not wasted.

"No doubt," Clary replied.

"Without me, you'll have the place to yourself again. I saw your girlfriend leave a little while ago. You have a fight?"

Unwilling to share the details of her relationship with Jo, Clary merely said, "She only had so many days of vacation, and they were up."

Marissa nodded and looked at her watch. "I only have time to strip my bed and throw my things into a suitcase. My mother hates to be kept waiting. It'd blow her away if I was ready to go on time."

"Bring your laundry up when you're done. I'll be at the house."

Clary spent a few minutes walking around her house, trying to rid herself of the lingering idea that rodents could jump out at her any minute, and Marissa appeared a short time later with an armload of laundry. Without knocking, she came in, dumped it in the washing machine, and started the cycle.

She looked at Clary and smiled. "I know I was a pain in the ass, but I think I'm better now. Like, I managed to get to that job every day and after that thing with Dale in my cabin, I didn't cause you any more trouble. That's something, isn't it?"

Clary pantomimed tipping her hat. "I'm sorry you had such a miserable time."

Marissa shrugged. "You're the one having the miserable time." Her tone was without rancor. "I hope you catch the bastard who's giving you all the shit."

Clary caught her by the arm and looked straight into her eyes. "I'm no longer interested in catching the person. Things have changed for me, and all those awful incidents are so much water under the bridge. I just want to get on with my life."

"You mean you don't care who did those awful things?"

"I'd like to know, but I'm not going to do anything about it now. So . . . " she pulled out the word before continuing, "if you had a part in it, you could tell me and nothing would happen to you."

Marissa snorted. "Oh, sure. Like I had a way to catch all those rats and let them loose in your house. I don't even have wheels."

"What about the empty can of gas I found in the trash? You didn't use it to set fire to my shed?"

"Hell, no. Dale bought it to fill his motorcycle."

"What about my obituary, then? The description of the person who brought it to the newspaper office fit you exactly."

"Obituary? I don't know what you're talking about." She frowned. "You mean that envelope I delivered? I didn't have a clue what was inside."

"Who gave it to you then?"

"Some guy who came to the restaurant for a cup of coffee one day. Paid me five dollars to drop it off on my way home. Said he was too busy to go himself."

"What did he look like?"

Marissa shrugged. "I don't remember. Dale was waiting for me to finish up, and Ellen was yelling orders at me.
I didn't notice anything about the guy except the five dollar bill he had in his hand."

Clary believed her.

Marissa continued, "I know for a while you thought I did all that stuff, but it's not in my character."

Clary remembered their exchange the day Marissa had arrived. "Like jogging isn't in my character?"

Marissa grinned, remembering that first meeting too. "Yeah, well, maybe I was wrong about you. It takes one tough lesbian to put up with the crap you've been getting." She headed for the door. "I'll come back and put those sheets in the dryer before my mother comes."

"I appreciate that," Clary said. "I appreciate something else too."

"What?"

"You finally got my label right."

"What do you mean?"

"Lesbian, not queer. That's a step in the right direction."

"Yeah, well."

As she went out, Clary noticed that she was careful not to slam the screen.

After making herself a glass of iced tea, Clary called Norma Latham to see if she knew Gerald Kahn's telephone number. Of all people, Norma was sure to have it.

"He's got an office over by the police station, but he isn't in it much," Norma told her. "You'll probably catch him in his San Francisco office. I'll give you both numbers."

After she furnished them, Norma said, "Anything special you need to talk to him about, Clary?"

Norma never wanted to miss out on important news, but Clary didn't want hers spread all over town until she had made a definite arrangement with Kahn. She skirted the question.

"Nothing important," she said. "I just had a question to ask him."

Kahn was in San Francisco, and his secretary put her on hold for a long time before Kahn picked up the line. He sounded in a hurry and his "Kahn here" was garbled, as if he were chewing on something.

Clary got straight to the point. "I've decided to sell my property to you."

The pause at the other end of the line was long enough to accommodate a reading of the Gettysburg Address.

"I'm glad to hear that. What, may I ask, caused you to change your mind?"

"An infestation of rodents in my house, for one thing. You wouldn't happen to know anything about it, would you?"

"Why would I?"

"I just thought that it, along with the fire in my storage shed, the poisoning of my dog, and a couple of other little incidents designed to screw up my life, might have been your way of persuading me to move."

Kahn laughed and took another bite of whatever he was eating. "I'm afraid I have better things to do with my time than play tricks on people. Obviously, I wanted your place but not enough to perpetrate foolish acts that might land me in trouble with the law. I am far too savvy for that."

Or savvy enough to perpetrate them but not get caught, Clary thought. But it didn't matter now.

"When can we get together and work out the details of the sale?" Clary asked.

"Tomorrow morning? I'll have my lawyer draw up the papers today and arrange for the funding. I'll be by with a check about nine. Is that convenient?"

"That will be fine."

She hung up, wishing the time would come sooner. Now that she had divorced herself from the tremendous hold this place had on her and had decided to make a new life with Jo, she could hardly wait to begin. Plus, she was also looking forward to paying off her debt and giving Richard the money he needed for the down payment on Cal's garage.

Doris, looking haggard from her ordeal with her mother, came for Marissa a little after noon. Marissa took it upon herself to load her things into the car, while her mother walked to the house with Clary to pay the rent she owed for the cabin.

After making out the check, Doris said, "God, Clary, I don't know what I'd have done without you to look after Marissa while I was gone. I know she was a pain in the butt. I really appreciate it."

"She started out being a pain, but I think she's making progress. She's going to be fine."

As she walked to the door, Doris asked, "How are things going for you? I see that you still have the cast on your foot."

Clary smiled. "It's almost like an old friend by now. But, in general, things are going very well for me. I know you're in a hurry to get home. I'll put it all in a letter."

* * * *

At ten minutes to six, Clary called the garage, hoping to catch Richard and Cal before closing time. She was anxious to share her news with them, and dinner in a restaurant seemed a good place to do it. Unfortunately, unless they wanted to drive all the way to Metcalf, the Inn was their only choice.

When Cal answered, she asked, "Are you busy tonight after you close up there?"

"Nothing more important to do than watch the news over a microwave dinner and go to bed. Why?"

"I have some news for you and Richard. How about I tell it to you over dinner at the Inn? My treat."

"You win the lottery or something?"

"You'll have to wait and find out. Jo left to go home this afternoon, so I'm without wheels. Could you pick me up?"

"Sure thing. Be there in less than an hour."

True to his word, Cal, with Richard beside him in the passenger seat, pulled up to her door exactly forty-five minutes later. For someone who had his pick of vehicles to drive, Cal's choice seemed strange: a rusty old truck that looked like it'd been built during Gerald Ford's administration.

Richard got out, helped Clary into the front seat, and hopped into the truck bed for the ride to the Inn. Even after Cal pulled the ignition key in the parking lot, the engine continued to run, and he and Richard took turns explaining the phenomenon to her as the lingering chug accompanied them to the door.

For a week night, the Inn was crowded. A young woman with an overbite and the biggest breasts Clary had ever seen led them to a table by the window and dealt out menus.

Clary looked around but failed to see Ellen. Thank goodness for small favors, she thought.

The waitress stared over their heads and offered her invitation by rote. "Want something to drink before you order? Cocktail, maybe?"

"A pitcher of cold beer and three glasses," Clary said.

"Pitcher of suds coming up."

As the waitress turned away, Cal said, "Okay, Clary, what's the occasion?"

"Yeah," Richard said. "Cal told me you had some sort of news. From the looks of things, it isn't the nasty kind you've been giving us lately."

"Just the opposite. The news I have tonight is beautiful. Fabulous. Absolutely wonderful."

Cal's eyes bugged with anticipation, and Richard leaned forward, eager to hear what had prompted such enthusiasm. For a minute, Clary simply smiled at them, savoring what she was about to say.

"I, gentlemen, have decided to sell my property to Gerald Kahn."

Cal shook his head in disbelief. "You don't say. I had the impression that hell would have to freeze over before you'd let your place go, especially to the likes of Kahn."

Their waitress returned and plunked a frosty pitcher of beer down in the middle of the table along with their glasses. "Want to order now, or wait?"

"Give us a few minutes," Richard said impatiently.

"Up to you." She turned to the table beside theirs to ask about dessert.

"What happened, Mom? What changed your mind?"

"Two things. I finally got tired of being harassed and . . . " She drew out the *and* to add drama to what was coming. "And I found someone wonderful to share my life with, in Santa Rosa. I can't live in two houses, so ... "

Cal cut in, "This someone happen to be the good-looker who comes to visit, the one I saw you with in the garage the other day?"

Clary nodded.

"Well, I'll be damned," Richard said slowly. "You and the lady pharmacist."

"Me and the lady pharmacist," Clary said, smiling. Richard smiled back, shaking his head. "Well, I'll be damned."

With the two men smiling and staring at her, Clary reached out and poured the beer. "If we don't start on this," she said, "it'll get warm." She lifted her glass. "Cheers."

Cal and Richard met her glass with theirs.

After a sip, Clary said, "We are drinking as much to the two of you as we are to me. You know that, don't you?"

"How's that?" Cal said.

"As soon as I get my money, which should be tomorrow if Kahn keeps his end of the bargain, Richard will have the down payment for the garage. And that means that you, Cal, can clean out that messy desk of yours and start building those model trains you were talking about."

Cal ran his hand over his nearly bald head and let out a soft whistle. "I never thought the day would come. Thank you, Clary."

"And what about me?" Richard said to Cal with false indignation. "Don't I get some thanks, too? After all, I'm the guy who's inheriting the headaches, all those tourists with their leaky radiators, the long hours, the twenty-year mortgage."

Cal raised his glass to clink it against Richard's. "Cheers," he said dryly.

Richard leaned across the table and took Clary's hand.

"Mom, thank you so much. This is the best thing that's ever happened to me. I promise I won't let you down."

"I know you won't."

They ordered steaks with all the trimmings and a large order of the Inn's famous garlic bread. Dessert was fresh strawberry shortcake with real whipped cream. Over coffee, they talked about how life would change for them, how wonderful things would be now that each of them could realize his or her dreams.

Richard had just launched into a description of how he planned to upgrade the garage when Ellen Graham came in, stopping at the kitchen to check on orders before sauntering over to their table. Her toothy smile looked genuine, but Clary knew better. When Ellen smiled at her, it meant trouble.

"Cal, Richard, Clary. Out on the town tonight? To what do we owe the pleasure?"

Richard innocently opened his mouth to tell her the good news, but Clary cut him off.

"The three of us just decided to have dinner out, that's all."

Obviously, Ellen hadn't heard about her decision to sell, and Clary wanted her kept in the dark as long as possible. Why give her an opportunity to start gloating any sooner than need be?

Leaning over the table to line up the salt and pepper shakers, Ellen said casually, "It sort of looked like a party. It crossed my mind, Clary, that maybe you'd decided to replace your wardrobe, get some decent dresses to replace those tacky dyke clothes you wear. Or, maybe you're finally getting that ugly cast off your leg."

The unmistakable verbal attack brought a frown to Cal's brow, and Richard half raised up out of his chair, as if to physically defend Clary.

"Sit down, Richard," Clary said. She looked directly at Ellen. "The wardrobe stays the same, and the cast has at least another week to go. Now, why don't you go stick your nose into somebody else's business and leave us alone?"

The toothy smile expanded. "Sure, Clary. I'm only concerned about your image. It would be a shame for it to get any worse."

"How do you mean that?"

"Well, it'd be an awful thing to get that cast removed only to have another one put right back on, if you know what I mean."

"No, I don't know what you mean."

"I mean that if you don't get smart and sell your place soon, I wouldn't put it past some nut to go and break your other leg. That would be a shame, wouldn't it?"

With that, Ellen turned on her heel and waltzed across the restaurant toward the kitchen.

Not attempting to hide his anger, Cal snorted, "You don't have to take that, Clary. If I were you, I'd march down to the police station tomorrow morning and report that threat."

"Report it to who? Harry Graham, Ellen's husband? Besides, it isn't worth worrying about now. By tomorrow morning, the whole town will know about my decision to sell, and I won't have to worry about threats from anyone anymore."

"It's between now and then I worry about," Cal said. "Keep your doors and windows locked tonight, Clary, and call me at home if you see or hear anything suspicious."

He smiled wryly. "I'd hate like hell for anything to happen to my passport to retirement."

"I always knew you loved me," she laughed.

Chapter Twenty-two

After Cal and Richard dropped her off at home, Clary poured a glass of wine and put on her favorite CD. A pleasing mix of pianos, harps, and guitars filled the room, and she was caught up by the sensual strains of a waltz. Standing in the middle of the room, she swayed on her crutches in a stationary dance.

Pounding on the door interrupted her reverie. Putting her wine aside, she found John Munger standing under the porch light. Lucy crouched a few feet away, a growl rumbling in her throat.

"Be quiet, Lucy," Clary warned. "Sorry, John."

Munger made a show of looking at his watch. "I know it's late. Back in my farming days, I'd have turned in an hour ago. Something I'd like to talk to you about."

Clary hesitated. "Actually, I was about to go to bed. Can it wait until tomorrow?"

"It won't take long."

Without being downright rude, it seemed she had no choice. She swung the screen door open to admit him.

Lucy moved to follow, her head low, her body in a half crouch. Clary found her attitude curious, but then she'd been acting strangely ever since the poisoning incident. She'd get over it in time.

Munger wiped his boots on the throw rug inside the threshold while Clary cautioned Lucy to stay outside and shut the door. She turned off the stereo and settled on the sofa, indicating the rocker for Munger. He sat and crossed his arms. The confrontational gesture gave her an uneasy feeling.

Clary shifted uncomfortably and sipped wine. "I'd offer you a glass, but I don't think there's enough left for more than a swallow."

"That's okay. Too close to bedtime for alcohol." He paused. "Not for you though. Go open that bottle of bourbon you found on your porch after the funeral."

She'd almost forgotten about the anonymous gift that she'd found when she arrived home that day. She'd pushed the bottle to the back of the cupboard, intending to save it for a special occasion. Even if Munger had been a frequent visitor to the kitchen, he wouldn't have seen it. The only way he could know of its existence is if he'd left it for her.

As if following her line of reasoning, he said, "I thought it might come in handy. I could see how upset you was at the service. You didn't drink it all, now did you?"

"No, but I don't see - - "

She broke off as he reached into the waistband of his jeans, under his plaid shirt, and pulled out a gun. Slowly, he raised it until the barrel pointed at her chest.

"Get the bourbon, Clary."

"I don't understand. What's going on?"

"I said, get the bourbon."

The gun made a good case against argument.

With Munger close behind, Clary went to the kitchen. She had the weird feeling that he was playing a diabolical joke, that any minute he'd put the gun away and burst out laughing. But he didn't. They walked in silence, and she was painfully aware of the gun tracking her every step.

She balanced her crutches against the counter, opened the cupboard, and stood there, trying to buy time. She had no idea what was on his mind, only that it boded ill for her.

"Hurry up," he said. "Get the damned bottle down."

She pushed aside cans and boxes, wishing that the bourbon had magically disappeared, but its black and gold label showed at the back of the shelf where she'd put it. Munger spotted it too and reached over her head to take it down.

"That worked out fine, didn't it? It's a rare thing when something you need shows up like that, right on cue."

He made it sound as if they'd collaborated on stashing the liquor away with this very occasion in mind.

Setting the bottle on the counter, he reached to another shelf and took down a glass, hesitated, removed a second.

"I think I'll join you. We can pretend we're celebrating. I *will* be celebrating soon. You'll be doing something else."

Clary tried to steady the tremor in her voice. "What are you doing this for?"

"You don't get it yet, do you? This is about your property."

"I don't understand."

"With you dead, it will pass to your children. I'll wager they'll be willing to sell it to Gerald Kahn. I've made it my business to learn about Richard's interest in Cal's garage, and I'm sure your daughter could use some money too. They'll be happy, and all of your neighbors will be happy, too."

"But, I've already sold the property to Gerald Kahn. He's coming here with the papers tomorrow."

Munger's laugh was joyless. "Nice try, Clary Webb, but it won't work. You've been saying for the past few months that you would hold on to this place, no matter what. Why should things change now?"

"Because of Jo," Clary burst out. "Because of all the horrible things that have been happening to me."

"I wish that was the case, but you didn't bat an eye, not even when I poisoned your dog. Now, you've forced me to take stronger measures. Now, I have to kill you."

Clary felt as if he'd smashed her with a baseball bat. "You'll never get away with it. They'll find out and send you to jail."

"Not if it looks like you did it to yourself."

He tucked the glasses under the arm that held the gun and picked up the bottle with his other hand. Pressing his body into hers, he put his mouth against her ear. He smelled of laundry soap and sweat.

"You ain't drinking to celebrate. You're drinking 'cause of your lost lover. What better than a few shots of bourbon to drown your sorrows?" He moved even closer. "This wouldn't have happened if you'd stuck to men. A lot of folks will view this as the just desserts of a pervert, a pussy-licking dyke."

She could feel the heat of his breath against her ear as his voice wormed in.

Outrage coursed through her body, and she swung around, flailing at his head with her fist. She managed to connect with two solid blows before he stopped her.

"Damn you, you queer bitch." He stationed the barrel of the gun at her right temple. "Try that again and I'll blow a hole in your head so big they'll have to scrape your brains off the walls." He pushed her out in front of him. "Get back in the living room."

Once there, he shoved her down on the sofa and set the bourbon bottle and glasses on the coffee table. Gun at the ready, he deftly unscrewed the cap and poured generously, handing her the glass. "Drink up."

She took a tentative swallow, feeling the liquor bite her lips and tongue. Munger made a derisive sound and jammed the glass to her mouth hard enough to jar her teeth.

"You'll have to do bettern that. I don't want to be here all night. Think of it as a challenge - - four drinks in four minutes. I'll do the pouring."

Encouraged by the gun, Clary complied. By the fourth slug of undiluted alcohol, her head reeled, and her vision began to blur. "I'm going to throw up," she gasped.

Munger emitted a sound of disgust. "Damn it, stop then." He looked around the room. "Go get a piece of paper and a pen."

Zombie-like, she got to her feet, wobbly and off-balance, and made her way to the kitchen drawer where she kept notebook paper. Midway across the room, she slumped to the floor in an inebriated heap. Munger stood over her, shaking his head.

"Damn. I thought you could hold your liquor bettern this. Can you write?"

She attempted to focus her eyes on him, tried to speak.

Both attempts were unsuccessful.

"Fucking dyke," he spit.

He left the room, and she could hear him rummaging in drawers, first in the bedroom, then in the kitchen. He returned, boots resounding on the hardwood floor, and hovered above her. Reaching down, he curled her fingers around a pen, threw paper in front of her.

"Write down what I tell you."

She poised the pen over the paper and waited for him to begin, wondering what he had in mind but too drunk to ask.

"My dearest Jo," he began.

"Wha . . . why? Letter to Jo?" she asked woozily.

"Yours is not to reason why. Yours is just to - - well, you know the rest."

She recognized the reference to Tennyson's poem "The Charge of the Light Brigade." *Theirs not to reason why / Theirs but to do and die.*

When she failed to start writing immediately, he prodded her leg with the toe of his boot. Laboriously, she transcribed his words, aware that her penmanship resembled that of a third grade child.

"I love you more than words can say," he continued. "You have hurt me to the quick. Now I see that we can never be. Life without you is terrible."

Even in her alcohol-induced daze, Clary was amused at the maudlin innocence of the message.

Munger paced as he dictated, stopping now and then to find the right word. As he continued, she became caught up in his story of betrayal and conflict. She stopped writing to listen.

When he noticed, he snarled, "Keep up, damn it. I ain't talking to hear my own voice."

He repeated himself, watching her scrawl on the paper.

After a few more sentences, he said, "End with this. I must end my life. Love forever, then sign your name."

When she'd finished the last sentence, he said, "Read it back to me."

She did, slurring the words, lapsing into fits of hysteria over the ridiculous scenario he'd invented. He ignored her and threw an envelope down, ordering her to put the letter inside and write Jo's name on the front. Satisfied, he placed the envelope in a prominent place on the coffee table and stared at her.

"Poor Clary. Such a strong woman, held her ground, stood up to everyone. But in the end, love did her in. Got drunk and took her own life. I reckon Kahn and the Grahams will be totally overcome with remorse when they hear the terrible news."

Angered by his condescension, Clary struggled to her feet to confront him face to face. Munger watched, his

Jack Nicholson eyebrows cocked in ghoulish superiority. When she lost her balance and fell back on the sofa again, he laughed out loud.

She was overwhelmed with the debilitating effects of the alcohol. With superhuman effort, she managed to merge the three Mungers before her into one and focus on his face. She looked him in the eye.

"Won't work. No one'll bleve . . . believe it."

Munger ambled to the rocker, sat down, and crossed his legs, regarding her with the curiosity of a botanist studying a new form of plant life. "Why do you say that?"

"Karen."

"What about her?"

She took a deep breath. "Karen knows we didn' fight, Jo and me. Jo'll deny it too. Police'll ask questions."

Munger threw his head back and roared his joyless laugh.

"The police won't even be involved. Why should they be? Everybody knows that queers are fickle in love. They'll take it for granted that you and your little girlfriend had a fight. Especially with the note you're leaving."

"But when Jo finds out later, she'll speak up. So will Karen. They'll know . . . " She floundered to finish the sentence. "They'll know I didn' kill mself."

"So what? Even if the police do come into this, nobody wants to air their dirty laundry in public, not when it reeks of sex. Your precious Jo won't want to answer a lot of questions about you and her. Daughter won't either. Everyone will keep still and blame your suicide on your imbalanced mind. You've been under a lot of stress lately, what with your lover's death and the dirty tricks. People'll just think you had too much to drink and let your imagination run wild."

Clary glanced at the gun, which Munger had placed next to his chair.

"You goin' make it look like I shoot, shot myself?"

He reached over, picked up the revolver, and fondled it for a minute before laying it across his lap.

"Shooting you would be quick and easy, for sure, but that ain't what I have in mind. You don't own a gun. I checked with Harry Graham. Told him you seemed a bit despondent lately and said I worried you'd do something foolish. As it turns out, your foolishness won't involve a gun at all."

Clary nodded stupidly, fascinated with this madman's inventiveness.

"Besides, don't want your body ripening indoors during this heat," he continued. "It needs to be discovered quick so that your property can go to your kin and then to Kahn."

"So how will you . . . ?" Clary couldn't bring herself to finish the question.

"Kill you?" he supplied. "Being drunk, like you are, you decided to end your life in your swimming pool. If you float to the top, you'll probably be discovered in a day or two. If that cast pins you to the bottom, I'll have to discover you myself. Won't that be a nice touch?"

He stood up, brandishing the gun.

"Let's go. Don't bother with a bathing suit. We'll just put you in the deep end lock, stock and levis." He handed her the crutches. "Take care on the way. We don't want you falling down and bruising. Wouldn't look good at the funeral."

Helplessly, Clary walked ahead of him to the door.

Chapter Twenty-three

Clary juggled her crutches in order to free a hand for the door, which she managed to open a couple of feet before losing her balance. Her captor rushed forward to steady her.

"Do I have to carry you to the pool?" he complained. "Stand back and let me get the screen."

Clumsily, she moved aside, and he pushed in front of her and released the latch. He'd opened it barely an inch when Lucy came out of the shadows and rushed forward, her body slamming against the grating. Her frantic barks chopped the silence like hatchet blows against metal.

Munger sucked in a startled breath and leveled his gun at her. "Put the dog in the house. The easy way'd be to shoot her. If you don't want that, handle it."

Obviously, Lucy knew that Clary was in danger and sensed that Munger was the source. Clary understood now why the dog had been wary of him. Lucy had witnessed him torching the storage shed and letting rats loose in the house. Worst of all, he had tried to end the dog's life by forcing her to eat snail bait. It was no wonder that she cowered and growled whenever Munger came near.

Clary doubted she'd be able to coax Lucy inside, but she owed it to the dog to try.

She removed herself from the crutches and handed them to Munger. Using the edge of the door for support, she eased down on all fours. Pushing the casted leg out behind her, she inched backward, stopping after a few feet.

The room spun and the floor rose up to meet her as she braced her elbows to keep from collapsing. Munger stood watching, his expression a mixture of curiosity and frustration. Outside, Lucy continued to bark and paw at the screen.

"Don't say anything. Move slow," Clary told him. "When I call the dog, open the door and stan' back."

Munger nodded and reached for the latch, stretching to minimize his movement. His other hand held the revolver aloft, index finger pressed against the trigger. Clary prayed that Lucy wouldn't spur him into using it.

With as much authority as she could muster, Clary called Lucy's name. From her vantage point, she could see the screen ease open and Munger's boots under his cuffed jeans moving away. Crouched and cautious, Lucy edged in, her nose twitching at the scent of danger. As soon as she was halfway through, Clary called her again, adding a whistle for emphasis.

To her relief, Lucy bounded toward her, undoubtedly aware of Munger's presence but momentarily distracted.

Clary rose up on her knees and engulfed Lucy in her arms, showering her with words of praise. Unused to having her mistress at eye level, Lucy lunged and feinted, welcoming the physical affection she'd missed since Clary's accident. It took all of Clary's strength to keep from being knocked off balance by the rambunctious retriever.

Gradually, Clary decreased the energy of their play and ordered Lucy to "stay." Using the dog's body for support, she rose to her feet and raised a cautioning hand, reaching out to Munger for her crutches with the other. The minute he proffered them, Lucy let out a threatening growl, her hackles rising. Clary reached down and patted her head.

"Take it easy, old girl."

She took the crutches and eased into them, pivoting toward the door. Behind her, Lucy's claws clicked on the floor in her desire to follow.

"Stay, Lucy," she commanded.

Her neighbor held the screen open, craning his neck to keep an eye on Lucy. "You go out," he told Clary.

It surprised her that he didn't opt to go first as a precaution against a last-minute attack. The only reason to stay behind was if he'd decided to shoot Lucy and wanted Clary out of the way.

"Leave the dog 'lone," she said, looking him in the eye. "She's done nothin' to you."

Munger's lips twisted in a smile as he picked up her train of thought. "Not going to shoot your dog. Wouldn't fit my plan. I'd have to come back and get rid of the body. I've disposed of a few dead critters in my time, but I don't need no extra work."

He turned back to Lucy and let out a guttural sound designed to incite her. She lunged forward, skidding on a throw rug and slamming into the door just as Munger pulled it shut.

Outside, he prodded Clary's spine with the gun, and the two of them crossed the veranda. Descending the stairs, Clary stumbled drunkenly into the railing. As Munger reached out to steady her, he inadvertently knocked a crutch away, and she watched helplessly as it clattered to the ground below.

"It'll take us all night at this rate," he grumbled.

He tucked the gun into his waistband and peered over the railing. "Damned thing's lost in the weeds. Never mind. I'll help you along."

Crossing the yard, he said, "Thought about the lake, but I'd have to walk you in deep enough to get your head under water. You can barely walk on dry land.

Besides, someone might spot us. We want folks to believe you took your life all by yourself."

That conspiratorial tone again, as if he considered her to be a willing participant in her own death. Considering her inebriated condition and the incapacitated foot, perhaps she was.

Stepping over the uneven ground, Clary fell into her captor, throwing him off balance and losing her other crutch.

"You can do better than this, Clary," he snarled.

The comment struck her as comical. Not only did he want her to get herself to the location of her murder, he wanted her to do it efficiently. She began to laugh at the ludicrous situation.

"You're somethin' else, John. Anythin' I ca' do to help? Carry your gun maybe?"

She leaned into him, aware that she was hysterical but unable to stop laughing. He rewarded her misplaced humor by clipping her across the cheek with the butt of the revolver.

Her head spun as pain traveled from her jaw up the side of her face. Blood, salty and metallic, flowed into her mouth, and she wondered how many teeth she would lose as a result of Munger's anger. Not that it mattered when she was about to experience the ultimate loss of her life.

Munger snarled, "You don't think this is serious?"

Clary rubbed her smarting cheek. "Perfeckly series. I jus' too drunk to care."

"See how much you care when you're under ten feet of water." He looked furtively into the darkness. "Got to speed things up."

He jammed the gun into his pants and scooped her off the ground in his beefy arms. She flailed to escape, but he was too strong and too determined. Taking giant strides, he carried her the remaining distance to the pool. Once there, he shoved the security gate open with his boot and walked inside. The gate clanged shut behind them with the finality of a prison cell door.

In spite of the danger she was in, Clary felt giddy and detached.

"This's so romanic," she said into Munger's grizzled hair. "Are you dying to kiss me?"

"Like hell," he spat.

"You might find it titillating. Everyone knows men're fascinated with les . . . dykes."

His only response was to continue doggedly walking with her across the concrete. At the deep end of the pool, he stopped and looked into the darkness for observers, his eyes darting nervously under their craggy brows. He took a step closer to the edge, and for a moment Clary thought he intended to drop her in right then and there. Instead, he lowered her to her feet, gripping her shoulder to keep her upright.

"You're so damned independent, thought you might want to jump," he said. "Ain't for me to take away your pride."

Clary peered down into the dark cave of water. A shimmer of moonlight played on the surface, and she remembered the night she and Jo had met here. She wished they could have that night back to live over again. It would have given them so much more time to experience the love that had eventually followed, the love that was soon to be only a memory for Jo.

She looked up from the water into John's face. "D'you really hate me 'nough to kill me?"

"Don't hate you. Just disapprove. You can't be what you are and not expect that, now, can you? Decent, God-fearing people have an obligation to disapprove of the likes of you."

He leveled the gun at her temple. "Once you're under water, it'll go fast," he said. "Don't fight. Fighting will make it worse."

"John . . . " she implored.

He met her eyes with a stony coldness.

"Want to go in on your own, or should I help you along?"

He tightened his grip on her shoulder, and she knew it would take very little effort for him to shove her over the edge. She took a breath and hopped to the ledge, noticing the ladder traveling up the side of the pool from deep underwater. Her only hope was to grab onto it before the weight of her cast pulled her to the bottom.

Lungs filled to capacity, she set her good foot on the top rung and set the casted foot down beside it. Munger stood with the revolver lowered to his side, watching her anxiously. Her instinct was to appeal to him for mercy once again, but she knew it would do no good. She let out her breath and took another, knowing that the longer she waited, the less time she could sustain herself under water. She lifted the cast, lowered it into the water, and pushed off with her other foot.

The pull of the cast was more intense than she'd imagined. Sinking rapidly, she reached for the ladder, feeling the slap of metal on her hands as she slid downward. Once below the reach of the last rung, there'd be no hope. Frantically, she clawed to hook her fingers. Just as the ladder almost disappeared from view, she caught the last rung, feeling the pull on her lower body as the cast anchored. She secured her grasp with the other hand and rested.

She opened her eyes under water. Shifting waves of murkiness drifted across her vision, darker in the places where her blood mixed with the pool water. Hand over hand, she made her way up the ladder to surface for air. When she emerged, her assailant was on top of her in an instant, cursing and wielding the gun. She saw that he was holding it by the barrel, and she understood the reason when he raised the butt and brought it down on her knuckles. Her scream overrode the sound of crunching bones.

She slid down the railing, submerging herself to escape another blow. Looking up through the water, she could make out Munger hovering at the pool's edge, the gun raised to strike again. Irrationally, she gloated over the fact that in spite of his careful planning, he'd given himself away. When her body was found, the broken hand and the broken skull she'd inevitably end up with would prove that her death wasn't a suicide. Small consolation.

The cold water had cleared her head and restored a modicum of reason. Not that there was much to reason about. Her choices numbered two: Push deeper into the water and run out

of breath, or surface and risk another series of blows from Munger's gun. At least, out of the water she'd have a fighting chance. She climbed the ladder, eyes closed against the sight of the revolver's butt coming down to meet her skull. But when her vision cleared, it wasn't Munger with his gun she saw. It was Munger down on the ground with Lucy on top of him.

The dog's golden coat shagged wildly as she snarled and bit at the man's arms and neck. He flailed wildly, trying to throw her off, but each time he raised a defensive arm, she secured him with tenacious teeth, awesome in her anger.

Gulping in air, Clary hoisted herself to the top of the ladder. The cast seemed twice as heavy wet, and her hands throbbed. Pain and fatigue kept her oblivious to the details of her surroundings for a moment. Then, she saw Munger's gun, resting on the edge of the pool not two feet away. Expending more energy than she thought she still possessed, she hoisted herself out of the pool and picked it up.

"Lucy, come!" she shouted.

The dog heard her, but kept her grip on Munger's leg, reluctant to give up the prey. When Clary called a second time, Lucy bounded to her, wagging her tail in satisfaction and lifting her head for praise. Clary lavished her with it, all the while keeping the gun trained on her downed opponent. He sat up, hunched over in an agonized slump, and eyed her.

"Wouldn't shoot me, would you, Clary?"

"Don't fool yourself, John. I have the same reservations about killing you as you had about killing me. In other words, none."

He smiled deferentially. "Can't say I blame you. For a woman, you're strong."

"I'm just strong, period."

Under the moonlight, with Lucy paying close attention, Clary herded Munger back to the house and phoned the police.

Chapter Twenty-four

Her weary body sagging into her crutches, Clary watched Karen squeeze orange juice and Jo ladle pancake batter into a frying pan. In spite of the pain pills she'd been given at the hospital the night before, Clary's hand throbbed under the bandages, and her mouth, with several of its teeth dislodged from Munger's blow to her jaw, was off limits to anything but baby food. She ought to be in bed, and that's exactly where she intended to go - - - right after breakfast. But for now, she wanted to savor the security she felt here in her own kitchen with two of the people she loved most in the world by her side.

Jo's first attempts had come out gooey inside and black outside and had gone to Lucy, who'd wolfed them down with the gusto of the undiscriminating. Now, she sat at Jo's feet, waiting for more.

Karen rounded the counter with a pitcher of juice and motioned for Clary to sit. She poured three glasses full as they waited for Jo to join them.

"If you don't mind my saying so, you look like death warmed over," Karen remarked.

"I have a perfect right to look like death warmed over," Clary laughed. "I'm just glad it's warmed over and not the authentic cold-in-the-grave kind. All that booze and my struggle in the pool didn't do much for my looks, and I definitely didn't benefit from my night on Norma's lumpy daybed. After Harry cuffed Munger and had him taken away, he insisted I go stay with a friend, and it seems the only one I have left these days is Norma. She was a dear, but I'm glad to be home again, especially now that I needn't worry about anyone blowing up the house or letting loose a batch of cobras. With Munger in jail, I can rest easy again."

Jo came to the table with a steaming plate of pancakes and sausages. She'd driven to the lake early that morning, right after she received Clary's call about last night's events. She still looked a little harried, but even without makeup, she was beautiful.

Swinging into her chair, Jo forked up three pancakes, slathered on butter, and drowned them in syrup. When she saw Clary and Karen staring, she defended, "Well, all of this has made me ravenous. You can see how I might be somewhat nervous when I heard that my favorite lover had barely escaped being murdered. I shook like a leaf the whole way up here."

"I still can't believe it," Karen said. "John Munger always was sort of odd, but who'd figure him for a murderer?"

Clary sighed. "He's harbored a homophobic hatred of me for years. When Kahn offered him twenty thousand dollars to harass me, he jumped at the chance. Not only did it give him a reason to make life miserable for a gay person, he could line his pockets at the same time. The way the police have it figured, when Kahn realized that I wasn't going to sell to him, he hired John to see that I changed my mind. By his series of dirty tricks, Munger intended to frighten me into leaving. By the time he infested the house with rats, he thought I'd be desperate. Of course, he was right."

"Then, why did he try to kill you?" Jo asked. "After the rats, and with a little urging from me, you'd already decided to sell."

Tentatively, Clary sipped orange juice, wincing at the pain it unleashed on her loosened teeth. "Apparently, Kahn had instructed Munger to murder me as a last resort, but he neglected to tell his henchman that we'd struck a deal. That's what John says, anyway. According to the police, there was an extra fifty thousand in it for him if he had to resort to murder, so maybe he conveniently decided to forget Kahn's instructions not to go forward with killing me. I guess the truth will come to light soon enough. If the justice system works the way it's supposed to, both Kahn and Munger will end up folding laundry in prison for attempted murder."

Karen reached down and patted Lucy's broad head.

"Thank God for Lucy here. If it hadn't been for her, Munger's attempt might have succeeded."

"Just goes to show that procrastination pays off sometimes. If I'd boarded up that pantry window as I'd been intending, she couldn't have gotten out to help me."

Jo rose from her place and shoveled more pancakes onto a plate. "We'll just have to buy her a month's supply of steaks as a reward. I have a big freezer in my garage and, as soon as we get to Santa Rosa, we'll go to the store and fill it up."

Clary frowned. "Aren't you fogetting something, Jo?"

"What's that?"

"I no longer have a buyer for my property. Kahn isn't going to be doing much construction work from inside his jail cell, not on either side of the lake."

Jo's face fell. "That's right. I guess that means our plans for happily wedded bliss will have to go by the boards."

Clary took Jo's hand across the table. "Of course not, Jo. It only means that we'll have to wait until I can find a new buyer. Things will work out. With all the time it took for me to realize my love for you, you don't think I'm going to let you go now, do you?"

Karen smiled at the two of them. "Barbara would approve."
"Yes, Barbara would approve very much," Clary replied.

For twelve years, Rising Tide Press has brought you the best in lesbian fiction and nonfiction. We are committed to our community and welcome your comments.

We can be reached at our website:

www.risingtidepress.com

Now available from Rising Tide Press:

<u>By The Sea Shore</u> *by Sandra A. Morris*

    Sydney lurched to a halt at the kitchen door of *'The Shooting Gallery'*. She turned off the car and cradled her head on the steering wheel, seemingly in no hurry to leave the sanctuary of the BMW's compact interior. She chastised herself for following Jennifer when she left the airport. She had not been surprised that Jess Shore had been there. Harley had spoken with Meg the other day and knew that Jess and Buster were expected sometime that week. Just Sydney's luck that she had arrived when she did, running smack dab into Jennifer. Did Jennifer and Jess know each other, Sydney wondered. She couldn't imagine how, but one never knew.

    To make things even worse, Jennifer had probably heard the honk of warning Sydney had been forced to blast when the dark figure had darted from the bushes outside Jess's place, directly into the path of her car. Had she not veered suddenly, she felt sure, she would have hit the stranger in black. She would call Jess later in the day and alert her to the incident. Strangers, especially this time of year, and dressed like some movie of the week cat burglar, were likely up to no good. Sydney knew that break-ins in the off-season were a problem for Provincetown's summer residents, and hoped that all was well at Jess's place.

    Moving laboriously, Sydney crossed the narrow path to the door and entered the hub of the bistro, her home away from home: the kitchen.

    The usually comforting sight of the gleaming copper pots and pans, the redolent smells of hundreds of spices and flavorings and the barren quiet of the interior beyond failed to ease the tension between her eyes.

"Damn you Jennifer Eastcott," she seethed aloud. Your timing sucks, she thought.

She swore an oath and whipped herself into a flurry of activity. Sydney didn't like discord and was determined to pull herself out of her current funk. Whatever the special was tonight, it would surely be chopped, pureed, or diced to within an inch of its life.

Sydney showed no mercy, even as she cleaved into an innocent carrot, sending half of it across the floor only to stop dead against a sneakered foot. She squinted at the silhouette in the doorway, recognition dawning sickly on her.

"What are you doing here?" Sydney questioned.
"I have a message for you, Sydney," the voice whispered.
From behind her, too late, Sydney sensed the presence of another body. As she turned, a white-hot pain exploded across the back of her head and all went dark...

Also available from Rising Tide Press:

	TITLE	AUTHOR	PRICE
❏	Agenda for Murder	Joan Albarella	11.99
❏	And Love Came Calling	Beverly Shearer	11.99
❏	By The Sea Shore	Sandra A. Morris	12.00
❏	Called to Kill	Joan Albarella	12.00
❏	Cloud Nine Affair	Katherine Kreuter	11.99
❏	Coming Attractions	Katherine Kreuter	11.99
❏	Danger! Cross Currents	Sharon Gilligan	9.99
❏	Danger in High Places	Sharon Gilligan	9.95
❏	Deadly Butterfly	Diane Davidson	12.00
❏	Deadly Gamble	Diane Davidson	11.99
❏	Deadly Rendezvous	Diane Davidson	9.99
❏	Dreamcatcher	Lori Byrd	9.99
❏	Emerald City Blues	Jean Stewart	11.99
❏	Feathering Your Nest	Leonhard/Mast	14.99
❏	Heartstone and Saber	Jaqui Singleton	10.99
❏	Isis Rising	Jean Stewart	11.99
❏	Legacy of the Lake	Judith Hartsock	12.00
❏	Love Spell	Karen Williams	12.00
❏	Nightshade	Karen Williams	11.99
❏	No Escape	Nancy Sanra	11.99
❏	No Witness	Nancy Sanra	11.99
❏	No Corpse	Nancy Sanra	12.00
❏	One Summer Night	Gerri Hill	12.00
❏	Playing for Keeps	Stevie Rios	10.99
❏	Return to Isis	Jean Stewart	9.99
❏	Rough Justice	Claire Youmans	10.99
❏	Shadows After Dark	Ouida Crozier	9.95
❏	Side Dish	Kim Taylor	11.99
❏	Storm Rising	Linda Kay Silva	12.00
❏	Sweet Bitter Love	Rita Schiano	10.99
❏	Taking Risks	Judith McDaniel	12.00
❏	The Deposition	Katherine Kreuter	12.00
❏	Tropical Storm	Linda Kay Silva	11.99
❏	Undercurrents	Laurel Mills	12.00
❏	Warriors of Isis	Jean Stewart	11.99
❏	When It's Love	Beverly Shearer	12.00

Please send me the books I have checked. I have enclosed a check or money order (not cash], plus $4 for the first book and $1 for each additional book to cover shipping and handling.

Name (please print)_____

Address_____

City _____ State _____ Zip _____

AZ residents, please add 7% tax to total.

RISING TIDE PRESS, PO BOX 30457, TUCSON AZ 85751